A FIENDISH ROAR

SURVIVAL IN THE STONE AGE IS TRICKY WHEN A DRAGON LIVES NEARBY

By

John Roberts

Copyright © John Roberts 2022
This book is sold subject to the condition that it shall not, by way of trade or otherwise, be lent, resold, hired out, or otherwise circulated without the publisher's prior consent in any form of binding or cover other than that in which it is published and without a similar condition including this condition being imposed on the subsequent publisher.
The moral right of John Roberts has been asserted.
ISBN: 9798443871592

This is a work of fiction. Names, characters, businesses, organisations, places, events and incidents either are the product of the author's imagination or are used fictitiously. Any resemblance to actual persons, living or dead, events, or locales is entirely coincidental.

CONTENTS

CHAPTER 1 *An Uninvited Guest* 1
CHAPTER 2 *The Settlement* 5
CHAPTER 3 *The Square of Yew* 9
CHAPTER 4 *Our Dragon* 18
CHAPTER 5 *A Local Disagreement* 21
CHAPTER 6 *A Trip to the River* 25
CHAPTER 7 *Another Square of Yew* 29
CHAPTER 8 *A Day's Hunting* 35
CHAPTER 9 *Cadwr's Story* 39
CHAPTER 10 *Siting a Rock* 42
CHAPTER 11 *A Night With Adain* 47
CHAPTER 12 *Finding a Rock* 50
CHAPTER 13 *The Woodsman* 53
CHAPTER 14 *A Short Distance* 56
CHAPTER 15 *Pulling Together* 59
CHAPTER 16 *Tree Climbers* 63
CHAPTER 17 *Crack Pot* 66
CHAPTER 18 *The Big Day* 69
CHAPTER 19 *The Long Wait* 73
CHAPTER 20 *A Day at the Beach* 76
CHAPTER 21 *Dead Reckoning* 79
CHAPTER 22 *The Thoughts of a Dragon* 85
CHAPTER 23 *What Next?* 87
CHAPTER 24 *Atonement* 91
CHAPTER 25 *From the Tops of the Trees* 96
CHAPTER 26 *Whither the Weather?* 100
CHAPTER 27 *After the Storm* 104
CHAPTER 28 *Boar Roast* 108
CHAPTER 29 *The Deadly Curse* 114
CHAPTER 30 *Dicing With Death* 118
CHAPTER 31 *Caddoc's Love and Loss* 122
CHAPTER 32 *A New Leader* 126

CHAPTER 33 *A Cold Wind* *131*
CHAPTER 34 *A Time for Revenge* *137*
CHAPTER 35 *Manhunt* *140*
CHAPTER 36 *Hell's Teeth* *144*
CHAPTER 37 *Heavens Above* *149*
CHAPTER 38 *Healing Wounds* *152*
CHAPTER 39 *On Manoeuvres* *156*
CHAPTER 40 *Poisoned Chalice* *160*
CHAPTER 41 *Beside the Lake* *166*
CHAPTER 42 *A View from the Woods* *173*
CHAPTER 43 *Another Big Day* *179*
CHAPTER 44 *Approach With Caution* *183*
CHAPTER 45 *Crying Wolf* *189*
CHAPTER 46 *False Hope* *193*
CHAPTER 47 *Save Your Breath* *197*
CHAPTER 48 *Follow My Lead* *203*
CHAPTER 49 *Decision Time* *207*
CHAPTER 50 *The Stone Age Diet* *212*
CHAPTER 51 *Running Home* *216*
CHAPTER 52 *Storm Clouds* *221*
CHAPTER 53 *An Act of Faith* *226*
ABOUT THE AUTHOR 230

To May and Mary
(and everyone else who has helped me along the way)

CHAPTER 1
An Uninvited Guest

"Hello. My name is Cadwr and I have come to kill your dragon."

Seventeen souls faced the lone rider. He was soon spotted as he picked his way across the open stretch between the forest and the headland. They were not taking any chances. Two young women had spears at the ready, whilst several elders and children concealed stones in their hands. A ridden horse was a rare sight in these parts. Nobody spoke as he dismounted. Eyes shifted nervously between horse and man.

They had never seen a dragon slayer before, but he looked to be an unlikely candidate. He was quite old, having survived well over thirty winters. Cadwr was very short at little more than one and a half paces and the few strands of hair left to him signalled the path of the wind. Unusually, he had a full belly and short arms. He did not seem to be much of a threat to anyone, especially a dragon.

The young men of the settlement were about four thousand paces away. They were trying to surround several elk feeding on the forest edge. The taller of the young women led the group in their absence. Her name was Adain. Until recently, Adain used to hunt with the men. She could run further at speed than all others. If an animal was wounded by spear, it was usually Adain who ran it down and put it out of its misery. Her man was called Gleis. He led the small settlement on the edge of the cliffs.

Adain was taller than most men. She had black hair and eyes of hazel. The slight bump in her stomach betrayed her recent labour. Already she wished she was fit enough to run free, hunting with the men.

Adain pointed her spear at Cadwr. "Where have you come from and why are you here?"

Cadwr pointed over his left shoulder. "I have travelled here from the mountains far to the north-east. All the dragons there have now been killed. Rumour has it that one still lives in these parts. I have come here to kill the last of the dragons."

Adain gently poked his belly with the tip of her spear. "Who has given you the right to kill our dragon? Why don't we send you on your way and leave the dragon alone?"

Again, Cadwr pointed over his shoulder. "All the elders at the large settlement by the river want me to kill the dragon. The beast has killed people there and they want an end to its terror. If you had the chance, don't you want to see the dragon killed?"

"No. If he starts to annoy me, I will kill him myself." Her friends laughed. They admired her courage and felt less afraid. The children broke ranks and startled the horse by running around in wild fashion.

Cadwr was confused as he was usually greeted as a saviour. "Dragons are dangerous beasts. How many of you has he killed?" His faltering voice revealed that the meeting was not progressing as he imagined.

It was an interesting question and Adain considered her reply. She looked towards her mother who was holding a new-born child. Vala gently shook her head.

"He leaves us well alone and we don't try to kill him. He likes to scare us from time to time and he does take his share of animals that stray from the forest. We believe that we are best served by letting the dragon live in peace."

Cadwr tried to regain the high ground. "You are fortunate. If you lived in the river settlement, you would think otherwise."

"If the dragon kills people elsewhere, that is not our concern."

"The elders at the river settlement are concerned. They have told me that the dragon has to be killed."

Menw, an old man from the group, stepped forward. He looked towards Adain and her nod granted him permission to speak.

"Are you a sorcerer?"

Cadwr looked aggrieved. "No, I am not a sorcerer. You do not need to fear me. I have no magical powers."

Menw viewed the stranger with suspicion. "If you are not a sorcerer, how are you going to kill a dragon? Forgive me, but you look like you would have trouble killing a goat."

Adain smiled and placed her hand on the shoulder of the old man. "Yes. If we gave you the right, how would you kill our dragon?"

"Dragons have a fatal weakness that few people know. My father managed to kill many dragons before he became careless and was burnt to death. So far, I have killed five dragons. I want to be known as the man who killed the last dragon."

Adain wished Gleis was by her side. She decided to bring events to a close. "We will not allow you to kill our dragon. If anyone wants to talk about this further, tell them to bring a square of yew. You are free to leave."

Cadwr nodded and mounted his horse with some difficulty. He set off towards the forest and the river beyond.

CHAPTER 2

The Settlement

The settlement lay on a finger of land that jutted out to sea. Earthworks stretched along the cliff edge on all sides. This served two valuable purposes. It meant that the dwellings there were largely protected from the ravages of the wind. Small children also found it difficult to fall to their deaths. At the northern perimeter, a deep ditch provided some protection from human and animal intruders.

There was one large structure. The walls were built of lime stones. The long wall on the western side was around three paces high. On the eastern side, the wall was just over two paces high. The sloping roof allowed the rain to drain away. The roof stretched almost to the ground. Young pines were used as rafters. Animal skins provided a protective cover. Turf was placed on the top of the skins and the roof was firmly held in place by external wooden beams.

A hollow log jutted at an angle through the roof. This helped to clear some of the smoke when cooking was in progress or the fire was lit. This building was the meeting house. In cold weather, all members of the settlement ate and slept here.

The recent arrival of Adain's daughter brought the number

of settlers to twenty-five. There were six couples of breeding age, five elders and eight children. Five similar settlements were known to exist along the coast. To the north-west, at about four thousand paces distant, another group lived on the edge of a lake. The largest settlement known to Gleis and his followers was the river settlement mentioned by Cadwr. This was around fourteen thousand paces to the north-east.

All settlers faced the same daily struggle for survival. The imperatives were food, water, shelter and safety.

Danger came in many guises. Falling from the cliff or slipping from the rocks into the sea almost always resulted in death. Wild animals also posed a constant threat. Near the headland, wolves and wild cats were the greatest fear. In the forest and at its edge, all manner of wild beasts could bring life to a violent end. Disease was the invisible killer. The local dragon could also cause some anxiety.

According to the season, some food was easily gathered. Children could help when nuts, berries, fruits, shellfish or fungi were available. The settlement was well known locally for its skills in fishing. Just to the east, it was possible to follow a path down the cliff to the sea below. A narrow inlet provided an excellent opportunity to trap fish.

The inlet stretched for over one hundred paces from just below the base of the cliff. It was only about five paces wide in places. Towards the bottom of the inlet, two sets of pine trunks were dug into the sand on opposite sides of the inlet. Just after high tide, the rocks at the bottom of the inlet became exposed. It was then possible to lower a wooden frame to the sea floor, held in place by the tree trunks. The wooden frame supported a lattice of thin willow branches and stems of ivy. This allowed the retreating tide to flow through the frame whilst trapping fish that had ventured to feed towards the base of the cliff.

As the tide ebbed, three or four women would scramble down into the inlet and scoop up the fish. The lattice would then be repaired and the frame lifted before the next tide.

If the weather allowed, most of the men would spend the day hunting for flesh. Some of the prey presented little risk, such as wild pigs or deer in their various forms. Boar were dangerous in confined spaces. The pursuit of cliff goats brought obvious perils. The greatest prize, however, was aurochs. These wild ox provided plenty of flesh, but were a real challenge to kill. They were strong, swift and wielded fearsome horns.

There were two main ways to kill an auroch. If a group of hunters could get close enough, a concerted assault was possible. The hunters would run full tilt at their prey and hurl their spears into its neck or flanks. This was only the start. The auroch would then lose its temper and start trying to gore anyone in its wake. The hunters needed to fall back, regroup and then attack again with more spears. With luck, perseverance and agility would win the day.

The other way to kill an auroch was by baiting a well laid trap. A large, deep pit was dug and thin strips of wood were placed over the opening. Sometimes, a sinkhole could be used, thus avoiding many days of digging. The opening was concealed by using the surrounding ground cover, such as heather or grass.

A brave hunter was then needed to encourage the auroch to pursue him. As the chase developed, several hunters would appear at the far edge of the pit, waving and shouting. If the auroch obliged, it would stampede into the pit and meet its death. If for some reason it steered clear of the pit, the outcome was uncertain. Sadly, death by auroch was not an unusual occurrence.

The greatest threat to the settlement was a prolonged spell of severe weather. Sea storms meant that fishing at the inlet was too dangerous. Animals would seek shelter deep in the forest from high winds and driving rain. A hunting party in a marshy, dark forest was a group in extreme danger. Without fish or meat, hunger set in within a few days of stores being exhausted. Twenty days of extreme weather placed life on the edge.

The settlers along the coast met up occasionally to trade or to find a mate. Trouble with neighbours was rare as life was difficult enough without the indulgence of local disputes.

CHAPTER 3
The Square of Yew

Three days after Cadwr's visit, two men were seen approaching the settlement from the north-east. Carrying spears, they trotted purposefully towards their destination. Every few hundred paces, they would pause to check their bearings and the terrain ahead.

It was late morning. Adain and several others watched as they hopped clear of the heather and crossed the grassy strip near the headland. They walked the short distance to the edge of the settlement. As a sign of friendship, they put down their spears and waited. The settlers were expecting a visit and the sighting of the two men caused little concern. Adain, her mother and several other elders went to meet them.

"Hello. My name is Sel. This is my friend Eus. We wish to speak with Gleis."

Adain asked if they were in need of food or water. Both shook their heads. "Gleis is hunting with some of our men. I lead our group while he is away. What do you want?"

"We have come from our settlement near the river at Carw. Our leader Caddoc would like to visit here to discuss your dragon."

Adain smiled. "We do call him our dragon, but he comes and goes as he pleases. When does Caddoc wish to visit?"

"He wishes to visit the day after tomorrow. He will set off at daybreak and he should reach here by middle to late morning."

Adain nodded. "And how many will travel to this meeting?"

Sel thought before replying. "There will be four of us. Eus and I will travel with Caddoc and Addolgar."

Adain had heard of Caddoc but his companion was not known to her. "Who is Addolgar?"

"Addolgar is an elder at our settlement. He offers counsel to Caddoc on important matters."

"I thought that was the job of his woman, Dera."

Eus laughed but continued to say nothing.

Sel smiled. "I do not know if Dera offers good advice to Caddoc. I do know that we all listen to Addolgar and his views command great respect."

"We will listen to what he has to say. Tell Caddoc that your visit is welcome. If you want to spend the night, you can all stay with us in the meeting house."

Sel thanked Adain. "We hope to visit and return on the same day. We will meet again the day after tomorrow."

Adain walked with them to where their spears lay on the ground. She picked them up and handed them over. All three nodded to each other. The two men set off at a gentle running pace to the north-east.

Two days later, all preparations for the meeting had been made. Everyone at the settlement wanted to be present. Gleis was worried that the children would misbehave and disturb the delicate negotiations. Vala agreed to care for them outside. She knew that her daughter and Gleis would give her a full account of everything spoken.

Around the expected time, four figures were spotted on the horizon. As they approached, Gleis crossed the defensive ditch and walked alone to meet them. They exchanged greetings and all five trouped through the settlement to the meeting house. They were followed in by fifteen others.

In the middle of the meeting house, there were two sets of log seats facing each other. Gleis motioned for Caddoc and Addolgar to take a seat. He introduced Adain and they sat opposite. Sel, Eus and the others from the settlement sat on the floor all around those seated.

Caddoc was taller and looked to be stronger than Gleis. He seemed to be somewhere around twenty-five years of age. Gleis was a little younger and certainly looked to be quicker over the ground. Addolgar was much older but had great bearing. Both men from Carw were surprised to see a woman sat opposite them but made no comment.

Caddoc opened proceedings by holding out a square of yew. In itself, it was a humble offering. Four twigs of yew were bound in the shape of a square. Each side was just over half a pace long. Holding one side of the square with both hands, Caddoc held it out to Gleis. The ceremony was complete when Gleis grasped the opposite side of the square with both hands.

The square of yew was offered by a person who wished to discuss a divisive issue with another. Nobody knew how the tradition started, but everyone understood what it meant. There were two key tenets. Both sides were free to fully express their views. More importantly, no violence would break out if there was a heated disagreement.

Gleis was expecting Caddoc to speak, but it was Addolgar

who opened the discussion. "I want to thank you for agreeing to hold this meeting. As you know, we wish to discuss the problems we face from the dragon who lives nearby. We also want to tell you what we want to do about it. Finally, we want to listen to your views and see if we can reach an agreement."

Gleis spoke. "You are welcome to our home. Please continue."

Addolgar was surprised by the brevity of Gleis's response but quickly recovered. "I will start by telling you about our settlement at Carw and how your dragon has been causing us much trouble."

Addolgar was quite short and had a slight stoop. Despite this, time had been friendly to him, with a smooth complexion and a full head of hair the colour of a gull. His voice was quiet, yet he spoke with great authority.

"Some of you have visited our settlement. It is sited on the banks of a river. This flows west for about six thousand paces before reaching the sea. About one hundred and twenty people live there. Like you, we rely on hunting and fishing to stay alive. Your dragon has troubled us from time to time, but things have recently become very grave. In the last year, we believe that nine men, two women and a child have been killed by the dragon. Others have been injured, some seriously."

Gleis was shocked. "I find what you say hard to believe. He has never killed anyone in this settlement and we live less than two thousand paces from his lair. Are you sure we are talking about the same dragon?"

Caddoc spoke. "The dragon approaches from his home and after his attacks, he always heads back to this place. He also has a damaged tail. I know of no other dragon that lives in these parts."

Gleis confirmed that the dragon that lived nearby had lost part of its tail. "If there is only one dragon, why does he kill people at your settlement and leave us alone? Have you done anything to make him angry?"

Addolgar glanced at Caddoc before speaking. "Something did take place over a year ago. All our young men practice their skills at spear throwing. One evening, about twenty-five men were on the south bank, testing their distance and accuracy. The dragon took them by surprise. Some ran for their lives. Others hurled their spears and two are known to have hit the beast. One spear sank deep into the side of the dragon. It let out a hideous roar and snorted fire. The dragon managed to stay in the sky, but we knew it was carrying a serious wound. It flew low to the ground and headed south. We sent out a large hunting party to see if we could finish him off. Sadly, the dragon was nowhere to be seen."

The meeting then took an unexpected turn. An old woman struggled to her feet and approached Gleis. Her name was Eres and she was Vala's older sister. Eres's daughter and her man were both dead, leaving a son called Ysperin. Eres did her best to raise the young boy, with help from her sister. Eres asked if she could speak and Gleis granted her wish.

"Around a year ago, there was a group out towards the Lonely Sister rock, picking sloes. When my boy Ysperin returned, he told me he had been talking to a dragon and pulled a spear out of his side. I thought he was telling untruths and I smacked him around the ear. He told me he was speaking the truth but I did not believe him. I told him never to mention such nonsense again."

Eres started to cry. It was Addolgar who comforted her. "Do not worry. You and your boy have done nothing wrong.

Is he here today?"

Eres continued to sob. "Yes, he is outside with my sister."

Addolgar continued to reassure her. "Could you help me and bring Ysperin here? Please do not talk about the dragon when you see him."

As soon as Eres left the meeting house, Addolgar asked Gleis if he could ask questions of Ysperin and he agreed. Addolgar raised his hand. "I ask all of you present to remain silent when I ask questions of the boy. It is important we reach the truth."

Eres returned with Ysperin and was led into the circle of onlookers. The boy looked frightened and confused. Addolgar gave him time to adjust to the lack of light and the expectant faces peering towards him.

"Hello. My name is Addolgar. I wish to talk to you because I think you can help me. Would you like to help me?"

"Yes."

"How old are you?"

He looked towards Eres. "I think I am ten summers." Eres wiped her eyes and nodded.

"About a year ago, you were picking sloes near the Lonely Sister rock. Something very unusual happened, do you recall?"

Ysperin looked like he was about to cry. He said nothing.

"I know you were told to say nothing more about what happened, but this is important. Our safety depends upon you telling the truth. Please help us. Tell me what happened when you found the dragon."

Ysperin looked again to Eres for reassurance. Eres spoke softly. "Everything will be fine. Please tell this man what you tried to tell me."

The boy cleared his throat. "I was picking fruit, but

wandered off to explore. I came across a dragon lying in a bit of a hollow. The dragon had a spear sticking out of his side."

"That is interesting. And what did you do then?" The old man's soothing tone encouraged the boy.

"I watched him for a good while. He was in pain. He could not reach the spear with his mouth and he could not knock it out with his wing. The dragon squirmed and snorted and looked to be close to death."

"So what did you do?"

"I circled round and then slowly came at him from the front. He watched me with his large eyes. I told him I was only small and I was not going to harm him."

"You spoke to the dragon?"

"Yes."

"And what did he say?"

Ysperin's jaw dropped. "He said nothing. I did not know dragons could speak."

The meeting house echoed with nervous laughter. Addolgar smiled and raised his hand.

"What happened next?"

"I stroked his head and told him not to worry. I had to watch myself because he kept swinging his head towards the spear. I told him I would pull it out if he did not kill me first."

Addolgar told Ysperin that he was very brave. "Can you tell me where the spear was sticking out of the dragon?"

"Yes, it was in the fleshy part, just below one of his wings. The dragon had to stretch back his wing to let me near the spear."

Addolgar pointed to the boy's chest. "Do you know your right side from your left side?"

"Yes."

"Was the spear in his right side or his left side?"

Ysperin pondered before replying. "It was in his right side."

Addolgar wanted to be certain. He sank to his knees and drew a dragon in the earth with his finger. "Here is our dragon. This is his head and this is his tail. Which side did you find the spear?"

Ysperin knelt down beside him. "It was here." He drew a spear poking out of the dragon's right side.

"When you reached the spear, was there much blood?"

"No. There was something like blood, but it was part yellow, part green."

"And what happened when you pulled out the spear?"

Ysperin winced at the memory. "I must have hurt the dragon because he groaned in pain. He beat his wing and knocked me over. I held onto the spear and ran for my life. I did not look back. I ran past the group picking fruit and I kept running until I got back here."

"What happened to the spear?"

"Before I got home, I hurled it over the cliff."

"Why did you do that?"

Ysperin looked guilty. "I don't know. I was not sure that I was right to help a dragon."

Addolgar smiled. "Thank you for helping me. I believe every word you have spoken. Do you want to stay here or play outside?"

Ysperin did not need to be asked twice and he was gone.

Addolgar spoke to Sel and Eus. "You were both there when the dragon was injured. Did you see where the spear hit the dragon?"

Eus spoke. "Yes. The boy's account is true. He was struck below his wing on the right-hand side."

Addolgar spoke to Gleis and Adain. "Some years ago, I saw a dragon shortly after it had been killed. It had three serious wounds. There was some stuff that bled out of the scales, but it was not red. It was a mix of yellow and green. I am certain your boy speaks the truth."

The meeting house now became a place of gossip. Adain stood up and suggested they stop for a little food and water.

CHAPTER 4
Our Dragon

We have now met most of the key characters in this story, but what of our dragon?

The first thing we need to do is to point out a misapprehension. As our dragon is powerful, frightful and lethal, everyone believes that he must be a he. This is not so. Male and female dragons look very much alike. Luckily, dragons can tell the difference and perhaps that is all that matters.

Dragons do not have names, but on this occasion we will make an exception. She is a dragon that lives in what is now West Wales, so let us gift her the ancient Celtic name of Morgana. Her name means 'the edge of the sea.'

Dragons are solitary creatures. They do not feel loneliness as we do. They only meet up to mate or to fight or both. Their union is always brief and often dangerous. Dragons have no friends. If a dragon rears young, the offspring quickly leave to find their own place in the world. Some years ago, Morgana laid two eggs, but they never hatched. Large sea birds destroyed them when she was seeking food along the coast.

Dragons like to live in the mountains or on the edge of high cliffs. This helps them to survive attacks from humans and wild animals. Caught on the ground, they can be vulnerable. Once in the air, they are almost invincible.

Morgana chose to make her lair on a large limestone stack about one hundred paces from the cliff face. The top of the stack had eroded at its centre. When she lay down, she was fully protected by rock all around her. Nothing could scale the stack to attack her. No spear hurled from the cliff could harm her.

Dragons are not as large as you might imagine. They have long, slender, powerful tails but their body is little larger than a horse. They have a pair of arms and legs. Their short, strong limbs are armoured with sharp claws. Their heads are small and very strong. Their jaws can crack skulls and their teeth are short and sharp. A spear thrown at a dragon's head is a waste of effort.

There is very little flesh on a dragon. Sinew, hide and bone are its hallmarks. The dragon has two wings. The first membrane at the front of the wing is the thickness of a man's ankle. Each wing is extremely tough, like an animal's hide. It is strengthened by three sinewy spars, stretching back to a strong trailing edge. As we know, there is some vulnerability below the wings. Most of the body is protected by scales.

The long tail is its most potent weapon. The edging on the tail is like the horn of a wild beast. One blow would render most animals senseless. One gentle swish can easily kill a man. Morgana's tail was damaged by a bite from an enthusiastic suitor.

The normal colour of a dragon is deep brown, with a tinge of red on their chest. For some reason, they do change colour somewhat at different times. They can breathe fire, but only in short bursts. Dragons do not know why they change colour or how they can breathe fire. It just happens.

Leaping from a mountain or a cliff is a quick and easy way to get into the sky. Dragons never fly far over the sea as they fear they may be unable to regain land. When Morgana needed food, she often swooped down on animals and smashed them with her tail. She would then snatch them up in flight with her powerful claws. Sometimes, she would enjoy a roast by incinerating her prey. Near the cliffs, she occasionally fed on heather or grass if flesh was in short supply.

Dragons always feel vulnerable when they have to land for water. Normally, they only drink at night. Dragons have good eyesight and their hearing and sense of smell are beyond compare.

Humans are not seen as natural prey for dragons. Apparently, it has something to do with the taste. They enjoy half scaring them to death but rarely kill them unless they are provoked. If a dragon is attacked, it will pursue the assailants without mercy.

So what happened to Morgana after her encounter with Ysperin? When the pain receded, she knew that she had to feed quickly and then return to the safety of her lair to recover. She slowly made her way to the edge of the cliffs, eating heather as she went. She summoned all her strength and made the short flight to the stack. Here she rested and dreamt of a return to Carw.

There is one final thing you need to know. An angry dragon has a deep, guttural, fiendish roar. You may be hundreds of paces away when you hear it, but that sound will haunt you for the rest of your days.

CHAPTER 5
A Local Disagreement

Addolgar was worried about the journey home. He knew he would hold up his younger companions. If it reached dusk and they were not back at Carw, all their lives were in danger from wolves and all manner of other wild beasts. He was stood outside, chewing a piece of dried fish. He motioned to Eus.

"I do not want to leave here too late in the day." He pointed to the sky. "When the sun reaches here, tell me it is time to leave."

In time, they returned to the meeting house to continue their discussion. Gleis decided to seize the initiative.

"Earlier, I asked why the dragon has attacked you and left us alone. I do not know what is in the mind of a dragon, but he has good reason to attack you rather than us. One of your men almost killed him and a boy from here probably saved his life. Men bear grudges when someone tries to kill them and favour those that help them. Perhaps dragons think the same way."

Addolgar spoke. "I, too, have had the same thought. The dragon has attacked our settlement far more often since the incident with the spear. Before then, he had only killed two people that we can remember. Before the dragon was injured, why did he kill two people at our settlement and no person from here?"

Adain stood up. "Our dragon is a good neighbour and knows that I would kill him if he started any trouble."

Gleis laughed with the others and playfully told her to sit down.

The truth was that Morgana enjoyed the sound of human voices. Her hearing was so acute that their chatter could easily be heard when she rested on her needle of rock. Of course, she had no idea of what was being said, but it was a comfort. She especially liked to listen to the laughter and shrieks of children. Perhaps their voices stirred a deep, maternal instinct and provided solace for the offspring she never raised.

There was also the question of hunting rights. The settlement on the cliffs was small and offered no threat to Morgana. Her favourite hunting grounds were to the east of the settlement, where the terrain was flatter and more open. As the settlement at Carw grew, more hunters were heading towards the coast in search of prey. Killing the occasional settler from Carw was her way of protecting the food supply.

Addolgar sensed that Caddoc was growing impatient. He decided to say what was on Caddoc's mind without causing too much offence. He stood up.

"Talking about what is in the mind of a dragon is not going to sort out this problem. The fact remains that your dragon is killing our people and he shows no sign of stopping. The only way we can see an end to this problem is to kill the dragon."

Gleis stood to his feet. "We respect what you say. The fact remains that he is not killing us and we do not want to provoke him in any way." His fellow settlers banged their hands on the floor in approval.

The discussion now became more heated. Caddoc offered a veiled threat about the size of their two settlements and hoped that a peaceful solution could be found. Adain did not like threats, veiled or otherwise. She jumped to her feet.

"If you attempt to kill the dragon and fail, both our settlements will suffer greatly. He will surely seek to exact a terrible revenge. I have seen your dragon slayer and I think it is Cadwr that will end up being slain. Do you trust this man? Are you certain he is able to kill a dragon?"

Addolgar watched Eus as he slipped out of the meeting house to check the position of the sun. He stood up.

"We have made some progress. We now understand each other's position. I wish to make a suggestion. We invite you to a meeting at Carw. This would give you the chance to speak with the dragon slayer. I am sure that we can reach an agreement that suits us both."

Gleis stood up. "If we visit Carw, I ask that the meeting be among no more than six people from each settlement. I also want to delay a final decision until I have talked it through with everyone here."

Addolgar glanced at Caddoc and he nodded. Addolgar asked when they would like to travel.

Adain wanted to be at the meeting. "Gleis and I and up to four others will visit five days from now. We will arrive by mid-morning." She felt that she would then be strong enough to make the journey.

The four stood up and filed out of the meeting house. Eus and Sel joined Caddoc and Addolgar as they prepared for the journey home. They all accepted a drink of water before setting off. Gleis and Adain watched as they crossed the defensive ditch and followed the trail beyond.

Adain turned to Gleis. "Why did you limit the meeting to only six from each settlement?"

Gleis laughed. "The thought of speaking in front of over one hundred people scares me more than the dragon."

Gleis asked if she would be strong enough to make the journey. "In five days' time, you will find it hard to keep up with me and our daughter."

Adain put her arm around her man. They watched as Addolgar struggled to keep pace with his companions.

CHAPTER 6
A Trip to the River

The group set out at daybreak. Gleis, Adain, her baby, her mother Vala and two young hunters made good time as they headed for Carw. The baby was named Llio. She lay in a sling of auroch's hide. The two young hunters were Tringad and Caw. Tringad was at the head of the group. He carried a spear in each hand. He constantly watched for potential dangers.

About ten paces behind was the main group. Gleis, Adain and Vala each carried a spear. In his spare hand, Gleis also carried a square of yew. They chatted as they walked in the general direction of Carw. At the rear was Caw. He also carried two spears and spent a great deal of his time looking behind him.

The first part of their journey was uneventful. They spotted the occasional deer and a bear in the far distance. The terrain was fairly flat. Underfoot, there were large patches of heather and the occasional strip of grass. They steered well clear of clumps of gorse to avoid any ambush from wild animals. About three thousand paces into their journey, there was a warning whistle from Caw.

"Dragon. Sit down. Lower your spears."

The message was passed on to Tringad and all sat in the heather. As they turned, they saw Morgana gaining height as she flew eastward. They could see the muscular beat of her wings as she powered upwards. She flew along the coast and then turned to the north.

Sightings of the dragon were a regular event. She lived close to the settlement and it was common to see her journeying to and from her home. When she was spotted, the accepted response was to sit down and not move. It was thought that the dragon would not see them and if 'he' did, they posed no threat and would be ignored. So far, the strategy seemed to be working. Morgana often saw them sitting in the heather and ignored them anyway.

Gleis spoke. "I hope he is not heading for Carw, today of all days."

They stood up and headed towards the forest. Further to the west, the forest was dense and full of prey. The woodland between them and Carw was more open and easier to cross. It was more difficult to be taken unawares by wild animals. Most travellers passed along this trail in the daylight without alarm. Even so, few people chose to pass this way alone.

Before they entered the forest, Adain asked if she could pause to feed Llio. The rest ate a few nuts and chatted as she breastfed the child. They then set off towards the treeline. Gleis urged caution and they picked their way into the shade. They followed a well-worn trail that meandered through the woods. There was birdsong but animals were nowhere to be seen. In time, they caught sight of the river and Carw on its southern bank.

Near the river, the grass seemed to be brighter than the grey green of their headland home. Caw was only fifteen summers and had never been so far away from his home. He was astonished at the size of the settlement. He pointed to the large building, furthest away from the river.

"That has to be their meeting house. It must have taken an age to build such a huge place. And look at all those other buildings, what are they for?"

Vala pointed to the ten or so circular buildings between the river and the meeting house. "Those round houses are family homes. Elders, their children and their children's children live together. Each family works to help the settlement. Almost all families will have young men who hunt. Some fish, some cook and a few do things like make spears or work on animal hides. It's just a different way of living."

Caw had never seen a river before. He pointed to the line of poles stretching between the banks. "What are those sticks in the water for?"

"Fishing," replied Vala.

"How do the sticks catch fish?"

Vala did not know and was tired of conversation. "When you get down there, why not ask a young woman to show you how everything works?"

Adain giggled and Gleis told them all to get moving.

When they reached the settlement, Gleis was surprised that nobody came forward to meet them. A large group was stood around, looking at something on the ground. As they approached, Addolgar's arm was tugged and he turned to greet them. Gleis asked what was going on.

"In the middle of that huddle is a dead man. He was killed this morning by our dragon."

"What happened?"

"He left here with two other hunters shortly after

daybreak. They were heading to the open ground to the south. They were about three thousand paces from here when the dragon attacked. He swooped down and smashed the young man across the head with his tail. His skull is badly crushed. Do you want to see the body or talk to the two survivors?"

"No. I accept your story. Let us start our meeting. We want to return home today."

Addolgar nodded. "Follow me."

CHAPTER 7
Another Square of Yew

It was only thirteen days since midsummer. The days were long and fine. Gleis was expecting the meeting to take place in one of the buildings. Addolgar led the group to a set of wooden seats at the river's edge. A stone building was only twenty paces away.

"We thought it would be good to talk here in the fresh air. You know Eus and Sel. They will keep watch. If needed, we can shelter in this nearby building."

Gleis liked the meeting place. He pointed to Tringad and Caw. They would also stand guard.

Caddoc approached with two others. The two groups sat opposite each other. Gleis introduced Adain, his baby daughter Llio and Vala.

Caddoc introduced Addolgar, his woman Dera and Cadwr, the dragon slayer. Dera looked as though she too would bear a childbirth in the next twenty days. Both Dera and Adain resisted the temptation to indulge in baby talk until the meeting was over.

Gleis opened proceedings by offering a square of yew. Caddoc grasped the square and the dragon trading began.

Gleis spoke. "I am sorry you have lost a man today. I

know that something has to be done. I want to make two main points. If you want to kill the dragon, we need to be convinced that you can complete the task. I do not want to live next to an angry dragon, seeking revenge. Also, we cannot offer you any assistance or sanctuary until the dragon is dead. Your men must steer clear of our settlement. I will say more of this later."

Caddoc spoke. "What you say makes sense. If I was you, I would insist on exactly the same things. Let us start by telling you how we will kill the dragon." All eyes fell on Cadwr.

Cadwr stood up and surveyed his audience. "Dragons are tricky beasts. Luckily, they have a fatal weakness and I know what that weakness is. I will not tell you all my secrets, but I will tell you enough to show how a dragon can be killed." He scratched his ear before continuing.

"Dragons can smell things much better than we can. We have to be quite close to something before we smell it. Think about a dead carcass on open ground. We would probably see it long before we could smell it. Until we get within about forty paces, we probably don't smell it at all. This is not so with a dragon. They can smell things from a great distance. This can be their undoing."

He paused as if he was about to reveal his deepest secret. "There is a particular smell that drives dragons wild with excitement. We know that dragons are normally very wary and try to avoid landing on open ground as much as possible. When dragons catch this secret smell on the wind, they seem to lose all control. They have to seek out the source of the smell and feast upon it. This lack of caution is their fatal weakness. If you prepare a trap and place this smell into the middle of it, the dragon will fly in and end his own life."

Adain scoffed. "I want to know a lot more about this trap and I want to know a lot more about this secret smell. The whole thing seems fishy to me."

Dera laughed. "Perhaps it's a fishy smell that drives dragons mad." Apart from Cadwr, everyone shared the joke.

Gleis stood up. "I agree. We need to know a lot more about the trap. Some hint of this magical smell would also help. Also, how can we be sure that you are not a charlatan?"

Cadwr was furious. "I have killed five dragons and my father killed many more. How dare you insult me in this way?" He swore at Gleis and shook his fist.

Addolgar stood up and Gleis and Cadwr were persuaded to return to their seats. "We all know that storytellers travel the country and pass on tales from one settlement to another. Three days ago, such a man came to us. I asked him if he had heard any stories of dragon slayers. He told me about Cadwr and described him. He had visited a settlement many tens of thousands of paces from here where a dragon had been killed by Cadwr. He mentioned the use of a magical smell to trick the dragon."

Vala passed her granddaughter back to Adain and stood up. "How can you be certain that this storyteller is not in league with this man?"

Again, Addolgar stood up. "I too travel widely and I have met this storyteller before. I have found his stories to be reliable when I have checked the facts at the place where the story began. I trust him. Also, when Cadwr came to us, we told him we would kill him if he was not telling the truth. He is still here and he wants to kill the dragon."

Adain stood up. "You told us that you believed that this was the last of the dragons. If you succeed, you will no longer have a job."

Caddoc stood up. "We have told him that if he kills the dragon, he will be welcome to live out his days here. We will provide him with food and shelter."

Gleis spoke. "We still need to hear more about this trap and this secret smell." Again, all eyes fell on the dragon slayer.

Cadwr stood up. "I cannot tell you the exact nature of the smell. If I told you, anyone could kill a dragon and you would no longer need me. I can tell you that the smell is made from mixing two things that you are familiar with. There is no magic. I don't know why the smell works on dragons, but I can assure you that it does."

Gleis nodded. "And what of the trap?"

Cadwr produced a length of vine. "This vine is extremely strong and we all use it for binding. If you make a loop and raise it above the ground, a dragon can land in the loop and it will tighten as he moves forward or back. Once he is trapped by his legs, you can kill him."

Gleis shook his head. "Dragons breathe fire. Once our dragon finds he is trapped, all he has to do is set fire to the vines and he will be free."

Cadwr smiled. "I would set the trap near the edge of a high cliff. All the vines would be tied to a large rock on the edge of the cliff. As soon as the dragon is caught, the rock is rolled over the cliff and the dragon is dragged to his death."

"And who is going to risk his life by rolling this rock?"

Cadwr beamed. "I will. I have done it five times before."

Vala stood up. "I am still not sure of what you say. Can you show us these loops and how the vines can be tied to a large rock?"

Cadwr had taken a small sack with him. He took out a

small round stone about the length of a hand. He also pulled out a weaving of thin vines that looked like a cobweb. "Imagine that this stone is much larger, at just under two paces high." He then wrapped the stone in the net of vines and made several knots. "See, the stone is completely secure and can easily be attached to the loops."

Cadwr then demonstrated how the loops would be placed to set the trap. He also explained how a heavy boulder could be quickly released.

Vala remained sceptical. "You would need to be close by to release the boulder. If the dragon has such a good sense of smell, how can you be certain he will not smell you?"

Cadwr smiled. "I always dig a small trench to hide in nearby. I place a decomposing animal by the hole to hide my scent."

Cadwr seemed to have thought of everything. He spoke confidently and kept reminding everyone that he and his father had done this many times before. Finally, everyone felt that such a plan might work.

Gleis spoke. "We need to talk this through with our people. If we agree, we want this trap to be set at least eight thousand paces from our settlement. We also want nobody from here visiting us around the time the dragon is to be killed."

Addolgar spoke to Cadwr. "Do you know of a suitable site for this trap?"

"I had hoped to place the trap closer to his lair. I will have to walk the cliffs and find another spot. I will also need to find a suitable boulder, probably from a nearby beach. I will need some men to get it in position on the cliffs."

Caddoc spoke. "We seem to be close to an agreement. Gleis, I ask you to discuss our plan with your people. Cadwr will find a new site and work out when he will be ready to kill the dragon."

Gleis glanced at Adain and Vala. Both nodded and the meeting was over.

It was late afternoon when they returned to the cliffs. After their meal, all the settlers listened to a full account of what had happened at Carw. There was much discussion. Some wanted to leave things as they were. Finally, Menw asked Gleis for his opinion.

"The people at Carw are determined to try and kill our dragon. Even if we do not give our permission, I know they will try anyway. We cannot stop them. If it came to conflict, they could easily drive us over the cliff. I believe we should agree with reluctance to this attempt. We will insist that the attempt is made a long way from here. We will also insist that we have no contact with them around the time they try to kill him."

Menw turned to Adain and Vala. "Do you agree with the counsel from Gleis?" Both nodded and the second meeting of the day was over.

Before sleeping, Gleis said that he was tired of negotiations. He was looking forward to a good day's hunting tomorrow. Adain said she was going to join him. Gleis squeezed her hand and said nothing.

CHAPTER 8
A Day's Hunting

Adain was frustrated. Vala told her she had to feed her child and she was still not strong enough to join the hunt. Gleis sided with her mother and she knew this was one argument she was not going to win. She swore and vowed to be hunting again in the next few days. "If you don't like it, Llio and I will go out hunting on our own." Their laughter only darkened her mood.

Gleis set out with four companions. Penn and Seith were experienced hunters. Tringad and Caw were still learning their trade. The wind was from the west. Gleis decided they would head north towards the edge of the forest. The group would then slowly work their way to the west, keeping downwind of animals grazing out in the open. A few deer were all they needed for a successful hunt.

It was a fine summer's day. There was little cloud and a refreshing sea breeze. The hunters could taste the salt on the wind as they turned to walk along the forest edge.

About a thousand paces away, a small herd of aurochs wandered out into the open. There was one bull, two cows and two calves. The bull was a powerful beast. His skin was almost black, with a tinge of brown. He was over two paces high at the shoulder. The main weight of the beast was in the neck and shoulder. His hindquarters looked slender in contrast. The bull had long horns of almost a pace in length. These pointed forward.

The two cows were much smaller. Their skins were a reddish brown. The calves were less than one hundred days old. If the herd kept together, an attack would be highly dangerous. If they spread out whilst grazing, it may be possible to attack one of the cows or a calf. A cow was the ideal target. They were much easier to kill than a bull and they still provided plenty of meat.

Attempting to kill a bull was very risky. It only made sense when a bull was alone and taken by surprise with a large group of hunters. As bulls were so powerful and aggressive, most hunting parties found good excuses to avoid them. The key exception was late summer. In the breeding season, there were often violent clashes between bulls. Occasionally, a bull was so badly injured it could be easily finished off by hunters. Last year, one bull was killed by another. All they had to do was to cart off the flesh before the wolves took over.

When an auroch is first struck by a spear, it usually does little at all. It tries to make sense of what is happening by standing its ground. This torpor passes quickly and it becomes very aggressive. It will charge or kick anyone in range. Hunters must immediately strike with more spears. At first, spears are hurled into the neck and flanks of the animal. When the auroch starts to tire, hunters can approach and seek to finish it off. At this stage, the aim is to thrust a spear deep through the ribs. The animal now bleeds heavily and sinks to its knees. The end is then not far away.

A strange feature of killing aurochs is the reaction of other members of the herd. If they are close together, the bulls and cows will work together to drive off attackers. If an auroch is more than about one hundred and fifty paces from the others, an attack is met with indifference. Despite the baying of the animal being assaulted, the others take little notice and continue to graze. Gleis and the others knew this and used it to their advantage.

Gleis and his fellow hunters were well hidden by a clump of gorse, a common shrub on these coastal grasslands. The spiky bushes with yellow flower provided some protection from a beast on the charge. Seith was on lookout. The rest lay and waited.

On this day, good fortune was with them. A cow had wandered from the rest of the group and was slowly grazing her way towards the hunters. The bull was well over two hundred paces away. Gleis signalled the plan of attack. Seith and Tringad would attack the cow's right flank and the other three would attack the left. Penn was the best spearman in the group and it was he who would strike the first blow. Each hunter had three spears. One was held in the throwing hand. The two spares were clutched in the other.

The killing of the auroch followed a well-rehearsed plan. Men appeared from both sides of the gorse and attacked. Penn's first spear sank deep into the cow's neck. He peeled away to leave room for Gleis and Caw to release their spears. On the other side, Seith and Tringad also struck their prey. All five hunters attacked again in concert. The auroch now tried to gore anyone who came close. Gleis yelled at Caw. "Keep back and watch those horns." Penn nimbly came in from the side and thrust a spear deep into the ribs. The animal died shortly after.

Killing the auroch was only half the battle. The priority now was to cut away the hide and remove the best cuts of flesh as quickly as possible. The scent of blood would be picked up by wolves, wild cats and the occasional marauding bear. If they did not move quickly, the hunters would become the hunted.

Using sharp flints, four men set to work on the carcass. Caw was the lookout. Gleis told Caw to keep an eye on the bull. Penn gently tapped Caw with his foot. "And keep your other eye on anything else with teeth or claws." The men joked and laughed as they expertly tore away hide and flesh.

It took some time to remove the bulk of the hide and cut away the best strips of meat. Spears were then quickly bound together to form a frame for carrying away their prize. The hide was placed on the frame and meat stacked on top. Gleis, Penn, Seith and Tringad each took a corner. Caw gathered up the remaining spears and they struck for home.

Back at the settlement, the flesh was stored in the meat room. This was a small area at the end of the meeting house. Antlers were fixed into the walls. Meat was hung here until needed.

The hide was scraped clean of all flesh and scrubbed in sea water. The salt helped to preserve the hide. In time, the skins would be fashioned to provide clothing, blankets or roof cover. Small strips produced items such as pouches and slings for carrying offspring.

This had been a good day's work. They had brought back a good hide, plenty of meat and no hunter was injured. Sadly, it was not always so.

The following day, Gleis sent two messengers to Carw with the result of their deliberations.

CHAPTER 9
Cadwr's Story

Cadwr had lived most of his life in the mountains far to the north-east. His childhood was spent playing in streams and climbing large rocks and cliffs near his home. When he was fourteen, his father put him to work. His name was Mil. Slaying dragons ran in the family. It was Mil's father who first started to kill dragons using the secret mix. His name was Brac.

Brac's woman discovered it quite by chance. She often collected honey and enjoyed mixing it with other herbs in search of exciting new tastes. One day, she decided to use sorrel to establish how its tart, bitter taste reacted with the sweetness of honey. She was outside, playing with her ingredients, when baby Mil started to cry. She took him inside their small home and started to comfort him. Suddenly, she heard a crashing sound outside. When she went to look, she was horrified to see a dragon gorging on her new mixture.

Fortunately, no real harm was done. When Brac heard about these strange events, he immediately asked for a new batch of the honey and sorrel mixture. He left it at a safe distance from their home and a dragon was soon lured to the spot. All that was now needed was a fool-proof trap and dragon slaying would suddenly become a whole lot easier.

At first, Brac thought it would be easy to create a dragon trap. He designed a pit but when it was tested, the dragon escaped. He tried placing the bait in a cave with a wooden gate that could be quickly swung into place. This, too, was unsuccessful and Brac's assistant was badly burnt. Finally, a friend suggested an ingenious plan involving the use of vines and a large rock. After much experimentation, a more efficient means of slaying dragons was born.

In time, Brac passed on the tricks of the trade to Cadwr's father, Mil. He became an accomplished dragon slayer and his skills were highly sought after. Sadly, Mil became complacent and this led to his death. It was a day that Cadwr would remember for the rest of his life.

Cadwr was with his father in a deep ditch by the boulder. It was a hot day and a swarm of flies was attracted to the rotting carcass placed near where they lay in wait. It was very unpleasant but they consoled themselves with the thought of one less dragon.

At first, all went to plan. The dragon landed on the loops of vine and started to eat the honey and sorrel. Mil released the boulder and the dragon started to be dragged to the edge of a cliff. The dragon was facing away from them and fought with his claws to slow down the slide to certain death.

Mil then made a fatal mistake. He wanted to show off to his son with an act of bravery. He jumped out of the ditch and waved and shouted at his victim. "Goodbye. We now have one less dragon to worry about." The dragon heard him and violently twisted round his head. Just before disappearing over the edge of the cliff, the dragon set Cadwr's father alight.

He suffered severe burns and took two days to die. His face was scorched beyond recognition and he could barely speak. He implored his son to avenge his death. Cadwr always remembered his last words. "Son, promise me that you will kill them all."

From that day on, revenge burnt fiercely within Cadwr like a dragon's breath.

CHAPTER 10
Siting a Rock

Caddoc asked Addolgar to make all the arrangements needed to kill the dragon. "Let me know what Cadwr needs to kill this beast as soon as possible." Shortly after, Addolgar held the first of many meetings with the dragon slayer. As it was a humid day, they talked in the shade of a tree by the river.

Addolgar told Cadwr of the decision to kill the dragon and asked him what he needed.

"I have to find a good site on the cliffs at least eight thousand paces from Gleis's settlement. I then have to find a round boulder of the correct size and move it to the site. I will need at least twelve strong men to shift it. Moving the stone may take a long time."

Addolgar assured him that he would get everything he needed. "And what about the vines?"

"I will choose them myself. Someone who can climb trees will be useful when cutting them down." Cadwr hesitated before continuing. "I will also need a large amount of honey."

Addolgar smiled. "Do you have a sore throat or is honey one of the secrets in your mix?"

Cadwr laughed. "I do need honey, but it won't work on

dragons on its own."

"I will not ask you to reveal your secret, but you must consider what would happen if you die. Your secret will die with you and we may never be free of dragons. Please think about this carefully. If you tell me the secret, I promise that I will never tell anyone while you remain alive."

Cadwr remembered the promise he had made to his father. "I will think about what you say."

Addolgar suggested that several men join him on his quest. They agreed on two men. A larger group may prove too tempting a target for a dragon. Cadwr said he would set out at daybreak tomorrow. Addolgar promised him two companions.

Very early next day, Cadwr set off from Carw with Eus and another young man called Olwydd. Addolgar had selected Olwydd as he knew the coastline well. He was also an excellent judge of distance. They headed due south and reached the coast before mid-morning.

Olwydd suggested that they walk out onto a headland. This would give them the chance to make sense of the local geography. Olwydd pointed westward to where Gleis's settlement lay. A little closer was the dragon's lair and nearby was a well-known landmark called Dead Man's Leap. Cadwr asked why it was so named.

Everyone in these parts knew the story of Dead Man's Leap. It was a narrow, steep-sided inlet formed by the sea relentlessly pounding away at a weakness in the limestone. The gash in the landscape ran inland for over two hundred paces. In several spots, the inlet narrowed to less than five paces wide at the top of the cliffs. The drop to the sea floor was over seventy paces.

Some years ago, two men were hunting along the cliff

tops. They disturbed several boar in a thicket and were charged upon. One of the men ran as fast as he could along the headland, pursued by an angry beast. He did not know of the inlet and reached it at full stride. He leapt across the gap, thinking it was of no real danger. The boar was not so lucky and careered into the chasm.

The man sat down to rest and waited for his fellow hunter. When he arrived, the two men went back to see what had happened to the boar. When the man saw what he had leapt over, he fainted with shock. He stumbled forward and before his companion could catch him, he fell to his death.

Addolgar had advised Olwydd that Cadwr would be interested in distances between various points. Olwydd continued his geography lesson. "As you can see, the headland meanders around, making distances a little tricky to work out. The best idea is to move a little inland and work out distances in a straight line. From Gleis's settlement to the dragon stack is just under two thousand paces. The distance from the stack to Dead Man's Leap is much further, about five thousand paces."

Cadwr explained that Gleis had insisted that the trap was at least eight thousand paces from his settlement. "Any site we choose must be at least one thousand paces to the east of Dead Man's Leap. We will take a look at the inlet and then pace out to the east."

When they reached the landmark, they carefully studied the drop and then Olwydd stepped out the required distance. A nearby slab of rock was chosen as the starting point for their search for a suitable site. The three men headed eastwards along the cliffs. Curiosity got the better of Eus. "What exactly are we looking for?"

"We need an open piece of land near the edge of the cliffs. There needs to be some type of natural barrier that forces the dragon to land with his back to the cliff. A thicket, dense gorse or a steep bank will all do the job. Just before the cliff, the ground needs to slope downwards towards the edge. The cliffs need to be high, with rocks at the bottom to make sure the dragon does not survive the fall. Look for the natural barrier first, then we can worry about everything else."

At first, the coastline was open and reasonably flat. Eus posed another question. "How close does this natural barrier have to be to the edge of the cliff?"

Cadwr smiled. "Very close. Fifty paces at the very most."

"If we cannot find one, I suppose we can always build our own barrier."

Cadwr was impressed. He had not considered this as a solution. In the mountains, it was easy to find suitable sites. "That is not a bad idea. Let's try to find a good place first. If we fail, we will think about building our own barrier."

The three men continued their walk. They were now almost two thousand paces from their starting point. Suddenly, they came across a sinkhole. It was deep and only about forty paces from the cliff edge. Cadwr looked happy. He rushed towards the sea. About seven paces from the edge, the ground fell away. The cliff was high. He peered down at the rocks below.

Between the cliff edge and the sinkhole, the ground was open. Weathered limestone poked through the grass in places. This should present no problems for the movement of the vines.

Cadwr ran back to Eus and Olwydd. "This looks to be an ideal site. All we need now is a large, round rock."

Eus laughed. "All I can see is grass, heather and gorse. There are no large, round rocks."

Cadwr shrugged his shoulders. "I am hungry. Let's go home. We will look for our rock tomorrow."

With the sun on their backs, they set out for Carw.

CHAPTER 11
A Night With Adain

The humid nights made it unpleasant to sleep indoors. Some slept in the open air within the encampment. Less adventurous souls still retreated each night to the safety of the meeting house.

The children loved this time of year. They made an outdoor fire and this was lit around nightfall. Their parents let them take it in turns to stand guard in pairs throughout the night. Each summer, the children were given a similar speech. "All our lives are in your hands. Stay awake when you are on guard and keep us all safe."

Gleis and Adain had their own little summer place within the encampment. It was a small, circular building made largely of stone. The walls were not sealed, allowing the sea breeze to cool the interior. The entrance was open.

Gleis had persuaded Vala to look after her granddaughter for the night. He had tried to be patient but he could wait no longer. He gently pulled Adain towards him and his intention was clear. She pushed him away and threatened to strike him. "Gleis, I am still too sore. I will tell you when I am ready."

"Well, don't make me wait too long. Your mother is becoming better looking every day."

Adain laughed. "If you mess with my mother, I will slice off little bits of you with a flint."

He grabbed hold of her and they playfully fought for a while. Gleis lay on his back. Frustration still seized him. "Don't talk to me again about going hunting. If you cannot tangle with me, you are not ready to kill aurochs."

Adain swore and laughed and swore again. She lay beside her man and stared at the stars twinkling through the gaps in the roof.

Gleis's blood had now cooled and he was drifting off to sleep. Adain had other ideas. She poked him in the ribs. "What will happen to us if that fat man fails to kill the dragon?"

Gleis told her to go to sleep. "If you don't want to sleep, go and fetch me your mother."

Adain giggled and gave him a hug. "I am serious. It takes a great deal to frighten me. If the dragon survives, I am afraid about what might happen next."

"I am not frightened. You told Caddoc and Addolgar that you would kill the dragon if he started any trouble. I believe you. I am sure that you can kill the dragon."

Adain giggled again. "I might need some help."

Neither spoke for some time. Adain continued to explore her anxiety. "If the dragon seeks revenge, what can we do about it?"

Gleis turned towards Adain. "I have given it some thought. Menw spoke to me yesterday and he also had several ideas."

"What did he say?"

"The meeting house is the safest place to shelter from the dragon. If we keep the outer beams wet, he should be unable to get inside or burn us out. We need to store more water inside. We also need longer spears in case we need to poke him off the roof."

Adain asked what would happen if the dragon kept on attacking them.

"We will have to think about leaving here and finding a new place to live."

Adain swore. "I like living here by the sea. I hope the fat man is as good as he says. Even if he does kill the dragon, I will still be sad. I like to see him flying in the sky."

Gleis sighed. "I know what I want but you just can't make up your mind."

Adain pushed him and laughed herself to sleep.

CHAPTER 12

Finding a Rock

Early next morning, the three men set out again for the coast. They headed to Pebble Bay, a beach about eight hundred paces to the east of the sinkhole. According to Olwydd, it was the nearest place that offered any prospect of finding a suitable rock.

For the most part, Pebble Bay was sandy. At the western side, however, there was an area of pebbles and rocks below the cliffs. Cadwr explained to Eus and Olwydd what he was looking for. His instructions were concise. "Find me a round stone about this high."

A boulder of the right size and weight was essential. Clearly, it had to be fairly round to make sure it kept rolling once in motion. If the rock was too heavy, there was a danger that the vines would snap before the dragon reached the edge of the cliff. A rock that was too light would fail to pull the dragon to its death.

In these parts, the rocks were mainly limestone or sandstone. It was not quite as heavy as the stone Cadwr used in the mountains, but the local rocks would suffice. A ball of sandstone that was a little higher than Cadwr weighed about the same as seventy men. When in motion, this was enough force to keep a sliding dragon on the move.

From a distance, the prospects did not look too good. The beach was well named as the stones were small. As they moved towards the mid tide mark, there were a number of rocks that showed some promise. The three men picked their way through the boulders, searching for their prize. Most were of no use as they were the wrong shape. The few rocks that were reasonably round were too small.

It looked like they would have to cross the headland to the next beach. Olwydd was relieving himself against a rock when Cadwr surprised him with a shout. "Well done. That may be just the rock we are looking for."

Olwydd looked at the rock more closely. Only about half of its smooth surface was sticking out of the sand. The stone was largely grey, with veins of blue. Cadwr found a piece of driftwood and started to dig a trench around the rock. Olwydd and Eus found their own tools and helped with the digging. The further they dug, the more excited Cadwr became. "Look. It seems to be round and it will be roughly the right size."

It was reaching the middle of the day. The sun beat down, forcing the men to find some shade. Eus scratched his head. "It is going to be difficult to pull out that rock from the sand to see if it's round and the right size. If we manage that, we then have to move it all the way to the sinkhole."

Eus looked up. He imagined a group of men struggling to roll a huge rock up the side of the bay to the top of the cliffs. Olwydd shared his misgivings.

Cadwr smiled. "I'm hungry. Let's go home. We will worry about moving the rock tomorrow."

On their way back to Carw, they saw Morgana in the

distance. All three immediately lay down in the heather. She had been hunting not too far away. In her claws, she held a deer. She headed for home.

Eus gave a wry smile. "I fear things are going to become a whole lot tougher."

CHAPTER 13
The Woodsman

As soon as his first meeting with Addolgar was over, Cadwr paid a visit to a craftsman called Alawn. He lived on the edge of the settlement, facing the river. Outside his home was a long, narrow workshop. He shared this with a tool maker called Neb. He made items such as hand axes, scrapers, wedges, cutters and bores. His materials were stone, wood and bone.

Alawn was a woodsman. Any project at Carw involving wood was Alawn's domain. Most of his working life was spent using timbers in structures such as homes, the meeting house and workshops. Cutting wood by stone needed both skill and patience. His father told him that a good woodsman always observed three key principles.

Always do the bulk of the woodworking while the timber is still green.

Always seek out the best possible tools to do the job.

Always employ others to do basic tasks.

Alawn and Neb were great friends. They worked side by side. When Neb was not making tools, he helped Alawn with his woodwork. Most cutting was done with hand axes of bluestone. Flint was not as plentiful and was only used for more intricate work.

In the hills to the north of Carw, there were outcrops of bluestone. Every forty days or so, two brothers would visit with axe stones they had fashioned from the rock. Neb told them not to bother to make handles for the stones as he preferred to make these himself. Neb was very particular. He would reject most stones as being unsuitable.

The brothers were well rewarded for their labour. They would stay at Carw for several days and eat with the families of the Alawn and Neb. Before their day's walk home, they were given some fish and meat.

Alawn had two assistants to help him with the hard labour. Efa was an orphan of around fifteen summers. She was happy to chop away all day at timber, joining in the laughter of the two craftsmen. Her companion was Drem. He was a little older. He was shy, but he worked well and listened to what he was told. It would be some years before Drem's feelings for Efa finally found voice. Occasionally, Alawn and Neb would lure children into the workshop to help with some heavy lifting or basic wood chipping.

Cadwr had learnt how to move heavy boulders from his father. He had a clear idea of how to move the rock and he shared these with the craftsmen. Alawn was keen to help. His brother had been seriously injured by Morgana. He fully supported the plan to kill the dragon.

He had never built a sled before. He listened intently as Cadwr drew sketches of the design. They were outside. Alawn and Neb stood in silence as the dragon slayer scratched his thoughts with a stick in the ground. Finally, he asked the two men what they thought.

Neb asked Cadwr how big the boulder would be.

"Hopefully, it will be round and a bit higher than me."

"Very big then." Alawn stifled his laughter.

Cadwr asked Alawn if he could build such a sled. He looked down at the sketches. "I have never made anything like this before, but I think it can be done. When do you need it?"

Cadwr grinned. "I will need it shortly after you have finished it."

Alawn nodded. "We will start straight away."

CHAPTER 14
A Short Distance

The three men set out again for Pebble Bay. This time they had company. Addolgar had arranged for eight men to help them to dig out the rock and check its suitability. They carried wooden spades, a collection of vines and three logs just under two paces long.

Cadwr also brought along his horse called Patch. To call Patch a horse was a bit of an exaggeration. He was really a mountain pony. Patch was not much to look at, but he was sure footed and very sturdy. His short, powerful legs meant that he could drag or bear a considerable weight.

When they strode onto the beach, it was just after high tide. They would have to wait for quite some time before they could get to work on the stone. It was already hot. Eus suggested that they retreat to the large sand dunes nearby. Here they could shelter in the shade.

Cadwr now shared his plans with the men. "When the tide has retreated, we need to dig out the stone and check if it is round enough for my purpose. If the stone is suitable, we then need to move it to the high tide mark. Finally, we will place it on top of the logs to stop it sinking into the sand."

In time, they all walked down to the beach to where the

boulder lay. The previous day's digging had disappeared. The tide had swept back the sand to encase the rock once again. A new trench was dug. While this was being carried out, Cadwr busied himself with the vines. A harness of vine was placed over Patch's head. Two long strands were laid out in readiness. The ends of both vines were attached to the harness.

When almost all of the rock was exposed, Cadwr placed a web of vines around the stone. The long strands were attached to the web and the moment of truth had arrived. Cadwr placed five men on each strand, behind Patch's back legs. "When I tell Patch to walk on, help him by pulling on the vines. Use your weight by leaning away from the stone."

When he asked Patch to move forward and the men pulled, the result surprised everyone except Cadwr. The rock easily popped out of the wet sand and rolled forward several paces before the webbing came loose. Some men fell over as the vines came away. Cadwr went back to inspect the stone. He was pleased with what he saw. It was not completely round but it would serve its purpose. He knew it only had to move a short distance to do its job.

The next task was to shift the rock just under one hundred paces to the high tide mark. Using the webbing, the stone could only be moved about three paces with each pull. Eventually, they reached their destination. With a little difficulty, they completed their task by leaving the rock sitting on a bed of pine logs. The pines groaned under the weight but did not fracture.

All the men sat in the sand under the punishing sun. "What next?" asked one of the men of Cadwr.

He was about to reply but Eus beat him to it. "I'm hungry. Let's go home. We will worry about moving the rock tomorrow."

Olwydd laughed and slapped Eus on the back. Cadwr muttered something about respect, yet seemed happy enough. Patch and the eleven men set off back to Carw.

CHAPTER 15

Pulling Together

On their return, the men received bad news. The dragon had again attacked a small hunting party and one man was killed. His neck was snapped by the thrashing of Morgana's tail. Addolgar asked Cadwr to meet with him once he had eaten.

They sat outside in the shade. Cadwr told Addolgar about the progress made so far. As soon as the sled was ready, he suggested that they start to move the stone. Addolgar talked about the threat from the dragon. He had noticed that the attacks were all made early in the day or late in the afternoon. Gleis had mentioned that the dragon had recently returned to the stack just after mid-morning and did not venture out again until well into the afternoon. Presumably, the dragon rested during the heat of the day.

To avoid further loss of life, Addolgar believed that work on the rock should only take place around the middle of the day. The shortest route to Pebble Bay from Carw was over open ground. By heading further to the east, however, they could travel most of the way through a series of woods. By posting lookouts and making use of cover, the risk of attack could be reduced. Cadwr agreed. He suggested that there should be two groups of men. One team could rest whilst the other worked at full rate.

The two men wished to check on the progress being made by Alawn and Neb. They were surprised to see the two craftsmen outside their workshop, testing a new sled. They easily moved it over rolling logs, dragging it with a length of vine. A huddle of children was placed on the sled to provide some weight. They screamed with delight as the wooden platform rattled over the logs.

Alawn and Neb greeted their visitors. Alawn described the key features of his design. "This frame will hold the rock. We will bind the frame with vines to keep it secure. As you can see, the rock will sit just a little to the rear of the sled. We think this will take some weight off the front of the runners and make it easier to drag."

Cadwr asked why they had removed the bark from the rolling logs. "It will make the ride smoother and the sap in the wood should make the sled move more easily."

The four men decided that the sled should be moved to the beach tomorrow. This was completed without incident. The following day, a large group of men and Patch headed through the woods on a long route towards Pebble Bay.

When in the open, they moved swiftly. At the last small wood before the beach, they watched and waited. Around mid-morning, they hoped to see Morgana heading back to her home. She was nowhere to be seen. Finally, Cadwr's patience ran out and he led Patch down towards the beach. The others followed, hoping not to catch sight of a troublesome dragon.

When they reached the stone, it was loaded onto the sled and made secure. Olwydd was confused. "The sled is pointing in the wrong direction. The sinkhole is back there." He pointed to the west.

Eus knew the plan as he had asked questions of Cadwr. "We are going to move the stone eastwards right down to the end of the beach. We will then move it past the sand dunes and along the track beside the small lake. When we reach the top of the track, we can then head back towards the sinkhole."

Olwydd remained unconvinced. "That's a long way round. It must be three times further than the direct route."

"Yes, but the slope on the track is very small. It will not be too difficult to keep the stone moving."

Cadwr joined the discussion. "Believe me, you do not want to be trying to shift a large stone up a steep slope like that." He pointed to the westward side of the bay. "I have seen men attempt it and it never ended well."

Cadwr split the men into two teams. Some men helped Patch with the pulling and the other team had the easier task of moving logs forward to the front of the sled. Every so often, the teams switched duties.

At first, the sand was flat and firm. They reached the far end of the beach very quickly. As they moved inland, the sand was much looser and uneven. Cadwr reckoned this was going to be the most challenging part of their route. They still had not reached the track when Cadwr decided to call it a day.

The following day, they had managed to move the stone part of the way up the incline. On the third day, there was a setback. On their morning walk to the sled, the men were attacked by Morgana. Fortunately, they were very close to a wood and they scrambled for cover. Several received minor burns when she set a thicket alight.

Shaken yet determined, they decided to continue with their

day's work. Five days later, the rock was near the sinkhole, at the edge of the cliff.

CHAPTER 16
Tree Climbers

Anwar and Eoin were both less than ten summers old. They were well known in Carw for their mischievous nature. Despite the protestations of their mothers, they enjoyed nothing more than climbing tall trees. They were battle hardened. Eoin fell out of a tree and was lucky to escape without permanent injury. Anwar had been attacked by a wild cat that had been lurking in the branches. He was proud to display the claw-mark scars on his back.

When he was not finding or moving a rock, Cadwr spent some time at the edge of the forest. He was looking for trees with long vines stretching up into the canopy. When he found what he was looking for, he did not have them cut down. He knew the importance of using fresh vines. With the sap still within, vines remain stretchy and strong.

Anwar and Eoin were recruited by Cadwr to cut down his vines. They asked why they should put their lives at risk for an outsider. Cadwr considered his reply. "If you help me, I promise that you will never be killed by a dragon." As they loved climbing trees anyway, this seemed a fair bargain.

Occasionally, the climbing vines could be removed by pulling them from the canopy. Mostly, they needed to be cut free by the two children. Neb had provided the boys with poles. At one end was a long shard of flint. These tools were used to hack away the vines from the tops of the trees. Cadwr stood on the forest floor, shouting out instructions.

When they had harvested a large amount of vines, Cadwr and the boys gathered them up and ferried them back to Carw. It took three trips to complete the task. Cadwr then had to braid long strands of vines to create thick ropes.

His technique was straightforward. Firstly, he stretched a vine between two trees. He then took a second vine and twisted this from left to right around the first. This was then bound at both ends. A third vine was then twisted from right to left around the first two. Again, both ends were then firmly bound to prevent the vines from unravelling.

Cadwr knew exactly what was required. Apart from ropes, he had to create powerful loops and links. He also needed to create a web of thick vines to wrap around the boulder. When he had finished his work, he went to see Addolgar. "I am almost ready. I have to set the boulder and dig a trench the day before we kill the dragon. Apart from that, I only have to carry out a few minor tasks."

Addolgar asked if he had a day in mind. "Let's say in four days' time. Do you have a rotting carcass for me?"

Addolgar said he had arranged for three deer to be left to rot. They were in different stages of decomposition. "You can pick the carcass that suits you best. I can get several men to move it to the sinkhole when you are ready."

Cadwr also checked that there was a plentiful store of honey. After his meeting, Cadwr gave some thought to gathering sorrel, his other secret ingredient. There was plenty growing wild near the riverbank. If possible, he wanted to collect this without attracting attention. He needed the sorrel to be fresh. The leaves then needed to be diced into fine pieces. He would leave this task until the eve of the big day.

Cadwr was content. Finally, the days of the last of the dragons were numbered.

CHAPTER 17
Crack Pot

Mair was not an attractive woman. Her face was wrinkly and she had no teeth worthy of the name. She was not very clever and her hygiene was poor. Apart from her plain looks, Mair was memorable for her hair. It was white and wiry and stuck out in all directions. Bits of bone and fish were often to be found within her locks.

Vala often joked that Mair had probably been struck by lightning. This explained the state of her hair and the state of her mind. Mair's redeeming feature was her good nature. She smiled all day and tried to help anyone in need.

Mair had two roles within the settlement. For two days, she would help those fishing at the inlet. On the third day, she travelled to trade with another woman from Carw. Both would set off at dawn and meet at a place called Flat Rock. This was roughly the mid-point between the two settlements.

The Flat Rock was hardly a landmark. It was a slab of stone that jutted out of the grassland by just over one pace. It was an ideal site to trade as wares could be displayed and exchanged with ease.

On most visits, Mair took along any uneaten fish. The old woman from Carw was called Nesta. She would usually bring river fish and items of pottery. Occasionally, one or both of the women had nothing to trade but they made the trip anyway. It was a good chance for a gossip. Both women were forgetful and topics were often discussed several times over.

Mair and Nesta travelled with several escorts to ensure safety. Gleis liked to send older children who were still too young to hunt. If messages needed to be passed from one settlement to the other, it was entrusted to their companions as the old women were hopeless with facts. If they remembered to report a message, it was usually twisted beyond recognition.

Addolgar wished to tell Gleis that the attempted slaying of the dragon would take place two days after Nesta's meeting with Mair. Sel was annoyed at being chosen to travel with Nesta, who was slow in every way. Addolgar explained that the message was important and Nesta was not entirely reliable. Gleis was aware that the attempt was imminent and he too sent a reliable envoy. Caw also wanted to be elsewhere but Gleis was insistent. "Listen carefully to Nesta's travel companions. They may have news of some importance."

When Mair returned from her trip to Flat Rock, Caw told Gleis about the planned timetable for the dragon. That evening, Gleis decided to provide a little light entertainment. After they had eaten, Gleis asked Mair if she had any news from the day's trading. Mair was not shy. She was happy to address all those present.

"Well, I took along fourteen of yesterday's fish. Nesta brought along five river fish and a piece of pottery. We talked and traded for a long time and finally decided on a straight swap. I was very happy."

Gleis humoured her. "Thank you. And was there any news of the dragon?"

Mair looked perplexed. "No. We never saw the dragon. We were not expecting him."

Gleis smiled. "You know the people of Carw want to kill the dragon. Did they say when they are going to make the attempt?"

"Yes."

"Yes, what exactly?"

"Yes, thank you."

Muffled laughter spread through the meeting house.

Gleis decided to try again. "Mair, when are they going to kill the dragon?"

Mair looked at her feet. "I think someone said something about it, but I can't remember. I think it is fairly soon."

Gleis tried to prompt her. "Is it the day after tomorrow?"

"Possibly. Is it important? I will be seeing Nesta in three days' time. I will ask her then."

Gleis felt that they had had enough fun at poor Mair's expense. "Thank you, Mair. Can we see the pottery you have brought back?"

Everyone was expecting to see a poorly fashioned piece of clay. With a flourish, Mair produced a bowl unlike any seen before by the settlers. Clearly, there was a new potter at Carw who had spent some time to create an item of beauty. Though the light was poor, the bowl seemed to be of uniform shape with a translucent quality. The rim was carefully formed with intricate edging. Mair held it up so all could marvel at its majesty.

Vala stood up to take a closer look. Unfortunately, Mair then dropped the bowl and it shattered into pieces. Mair sighed before flashing a toothless grin. "Don't worry. I hope you enjoyed the river fish."

CHAPTER 18
The Big Day

It was late morning. Cadwr, Olwydd and Patch approached the sinkhole from the east. They had taken the long route towards Pebble Bay and then crossed the headland.

The previous day, the boulder had been readied. It was placed on the slope of the cliff edge. The rock was securely tethered. The web of vines around the rock was already in place. A trench had been dug for Cadwr to hide in. A carcass was placed near the trench to hide his scent.

The plan was sound. While the dragon was resting, the men would prepare their trap. Olwydd and Patch would then return to Carw. When the dragon was dead, Cadwr too would head for home.

To save time, Cadwr and Olwydd had practised the layout of the vines. They unloaded the ropes from the pony and set to work. Cadwr paid special attention to the positioning of the loops that would tighten around the dragon's legs. Two layers of loops were raised above the ground by placing them on twigs. The layers were deliberately sited so that they were not directly above each other. If the dragon's foot happened to tread on the rope of the upper loop, it would still be caught by the loop below.

The ropes of vine stretched out from the loops near the sinkhole to the boulder. Five separate ropes were attached to the web around the stone. Cadwr understood the importance of spreading the load over a series of ropes. He was very confident that the vines would have sufficient strength to pull the dragon over the cliff.

Finally, a large bowl was placed between the sinkhole and the loops. It was full of honey and sorrel. Cadwr checked that everything was in place. Olwydd wished him good fortune and then headed back with Patch.

Cadwr made his way to the trench. He carried a water skin. He also had an animal skin to shelter from the sun. This was the hardest part. In the heat of the day, Cadwr waited a long time and started to doze off.

It was now late afternoon. Morgana was heading home to the south-west. The offshore breeze carried Cadwr's fateful scent towards her. She picked up the smell and was drawn to the coast like a moth to the flame. The hypnotic lure of the honey and sorrel drew her in.

She could now see the sinkhole and the large bowl just beyond. As Cadwr had planned, she flew past the sinkhole and came in low over the cliffs. Cadwr regained his senses just in time. Morgana glimpsed the boulder. She smelt the rotting carcass. She ignored both. Impatiently, she landed directly on top of the loops.

Cadwr crept out of his trench and crawled towards the boulder. It was secured by a thick rope of vines. Just two knots kept the rope secure. When the second knot was untied, Cadwr only had to unwrap a little of the rope binding for gravity to play its part.

Suddenly, the ropes rushed towards the cliff and the loops

tightened. Morgana had just started to gorge from the bowl when her legs were snatched from beneath her. She hit the ground with a thud and started to be dragged towards the cliff.

Her first reaction was to slow down her slide by digging in her claws. Her short arms stretched out before her. She ploughed deep trails in the turf as she desperately fought to slow herself down. She also tried to gain some traction with her feet. She was in luck. In places, limestone stuck out of the headland. She managed to catch one foot on a ledge of rock. She shuddered to a halt. She manoeuvred her other leg to secure her hold.

The pressure on her legs was intense. It was only a matter of time before she surrendered to exhaustion. Morgana's powerful tail now came into play. She started to thrash at the invisible force that was seeking to drag her over the cliff.

Some blows did little more than weaken the vines by flattening them against the grass. When her tail struck the ropes with limestone directly below, she could hear the ropes starting to sever. The fibres sang and groaned in response to the weight of the boulder and the thrashing of her tail.

Cadwr could not understand what was happening. The dragon had come to a halt just over half the way to the cliff edge. He could hear the deep breathing of the dragon. He could also see that the vines were being weakened with every blow of Morgana's tail. He took several steps forward to get a clearer view.

Finally, Morgana caught one of the ropes with a perfect blow. The edging of her tail severed it by striking the limestone below. The vines were stretched to their limit and finally snapped. At great speed, the vines snaked over the cliff. Cadwr heard the crash of the boulder as it struck the rocks below.

Cadwr now made a big mistake. He cursed the dragon. On hearing him, Morgana swished her tail for a final time. He saw the danger but was too slow to avoid it. The tail broke Cadwr's leg and lifted him off his feet. He was knocked out when his head struck a stone.

When Cadwr regained consciousness, he was in great pain. Facing the cliff, he struggled to his feet. He tried to make sense of what had happened to him. The boulder was gone, but where was the dragon? Cadwr slowly edged his way round towards the sinkhole.

Morgana was sat facing him. She was only about four paces away. The dragon slayer could hear her breathing. Her stomach rose and fell as she regained her breath. They stared at each other for some time.

Suddenly, Morgana drew a huge breath. Her nostrils flared as she sucked in air. Cadwr knew what was to come. "Just like my father." This was his final utterance before being enveloped in a huge ball of flame.

Cadwr sought relief by staggering over the cliff. His last thoughts were of his father and an unkept promise. The rocks below brought Cadwr's agony to a welcome end.

CHAPTER 19
The Long Wait

Tarran waited patiently for Patch to return. From the moment she first saw the pony, she fell in love. She followed Patch everywhere. She cried when they would not let her go to Pebble Bay. Cadwr had given her a wooden comb and showed her how to look after his mane. Tarran learnt how to feed and water the pony. She cleaned out his impromptu stable. She sought nothing in return. Being with Patch was reward enough.

It was late afternoon when Olwydd and Patch entered Carw. Olwydd handed over the reins to Tarran and sought out Addolgar. The elder was walking along the riverbank with Caddoc and Dera. Olwydd gave them a brief outline of the day's events. All they could do now was watch and wait.

Earlier, Addolgar had asked Eus to travel with Anwar and Eoin to one of the woods on the way to Pebble Bay. The boys would take it in turns to climb one of the tall trees with views over the open stretch between Carw and the sinkhole. When Cadwr was spotted, all three were to return to Carw as quickly as possible. A small group would be ready to set out and meet Cadwr. This would provide him with protection towards the end of his journey.

Two hunters returned to Carw from the east. They had seen the dragon returning home and reported that he had changed direction towards the sinkhole. There was still no sighting of Cadwr. Time was passing and concern for the dragon slayer grew.

In the woods, Anwar climbed down from his lookout and Eoin took his place. Anwar was beginning to get fed up. "How much longer do we have to keep watch?"

Eus too was starting to worry. "We will wait a little longer. Don't worry. We will return well before sunset."

Eoin had now reached the viewing point. Eus shouted up to him. "Any sign of Cadwr?"

Eoin scanned the landscape before him. He knew roughly where the sinkhole was on the horizon. He followed the route Cadwr would have to take as he made his way home. Apart from a deer, nothing moved. "He's not out there."

"Thank you. Keep looking. He must set out for home soon or the wolves will have him."

Eus watched as the sun gradually changed from a dull yellow to red. It was time to leave. Eus asked Eoin to take one final look. Moments later, Eoin started to make his descent. When he reached Anwar and Eus, he shook his head. They picked up their spears and trotted towards Carw.

Olwydd was now very worried. Addolgar and Caddoc were adamant. It made no sense to send out a search party this late in the day. If Eus brought no news, the chances were that he would not return before nightfall.

Shortly before dusk, Eus returned with Anwar and Eoin. The mothers of the two boys could not decide whether to hug them or clip them round the ear. Addolgar made a point of thanking them for their service. Their skills as lookouts may be needed again.

A fire was lit on a high point near the settlement. If Cadwr was still out there, the flames might just guide him home. No more could be done until daylight.

Next morning, Eus and Olwydd set out to discover what had happened to Cadwr. They took the safe route through the woods. In the heat of the day, Olwydd would travel alone to the sinkhole. Hopefully, he could find out what had happened. His aim was to return to Eus and the safety of the woods as quickly as possible.

CHAPTER 20

A Day at the Beach

In great pain, Morgana had returned from the sinkhole to her lair. She had a sleepless night. Her legs felt like they were bound in thorns. Her claws had been dragged from sinew and bone. It was as if her feet and arms were aflame. As the sun rose, she was in low spirits. She was tired. She was in agony. She was also very angry.

Olwydd quickly made his way across the headland to the sinkhole. He surveyed the scene. First, he examined the large bowl of honey and sorrel. Some of the mixture had been consumed and a small amount had splashed on the ground.

The previous evening, Addolgar had told him what to do. If the bowl was still there, he was to carry it to the cliff and throw it over the edge. He was warned to avoid getting any of the contents on himself.

Olwydd examined the claw marks in the turf. He noted that they only ran part of the way to the cliff edge. The boulder was gone. The section of vines nearest to the rock was gone. Most of the loops and some of the ropes were still scattered around.

Olwydd examined the trench. He had left a spear there for Cadwr's journey home. The spear was still there. His water skin and the protective skin were also still there. The carcass continued to smell. He tried to look over the edge of the cliff, but he could not see anything on the rocks below.

When Morgana was young, her mother had badly damaged one of her feet. To relieve the pain, she had flown to the nearest beach and bathed her wound in the sea. The distant memory beckoned Morgana to follow her mother's example. It was time to head eastwards to the nearest beach.

Olwydd gathered up the contents of the trench and set off across the headland. Morgana first spotted him from the sun glinting on the flint of his spear. She swept down towards him. Olwydd caught sight of her and started to run. She lined him up and attacked. As she opened her claws, the piercing pain returned. At the last moment, she broke off her assault. Olwydd threw himself to the ground as she swept over him. She carried on and disappeared from view near Pebble Bay.

Dazed, Olwydd picked himself up and ran back swiftly to the safety of the woods. Just before he left the headland, he had a view of the beach. He was astonished to see the dragon moving slowly through the surf. When he met up with Eus, he was too out of breath to offer explanations.

Back at Carw, Olwydd described the day's events. Addolgar, Caddoc and Eus listened in silence until his account was complete. Nobody spoke. Olwydd filled the void. "I have three questions. What happened to Cadwr? Why did the dragon not kill me? What was he doing on the beach?"

Addolgar spoke. "I fear that Cadwr is probably dead. Somehow, the dragon managed to survive. It may be that the ropes were not strong enough and snapped under the strain. There is only one question we have to worry about. What will the dragon do next?"

Caddoc remembered what Adain had said if the dragon survived. "We should try to let Gleis's settlement know that the dragon is still very much alive. Both our settlements may come under attack."

Addolgar agreed. "It is too late to get there and back today. The messenger would have to stay there overnight."

"I feel we must warn them. We failed to kill the dragon. If he exacts revenge, it is our fault. Who are our two fastest messengers?"

Olwydd nominated Sel and Naw. Eus nodded his approval. Caddoc asked Olwydd to seek them out as quickly as possible. When they appeared, Caddoc asked them to deliver the sombre message. "Tell Gleis that the dragon is still alive. Tell him we are sorry for our failure. Tell him we are sorry if the dragon exacts revenge. Tell him we will try to help if we can."

The two messengers grabbed their spears. They were handed a water skin and a pouch of dried fruit. Sel checked the position of the sun before leading the way at a steady running pace.

Addolgar offered some counsel to Caddoc. "We must tell everyone that we may be attacked at any moment. People should stay inside or very near their homes. Tonight, we all need to meet to talk about what happens next." Caddoc nodded. They both set out to spread the word.

The salt water had eased away some of Morgana's pain. The time had come for a reckoning.

CHAPTER 21
Dead Reckoning

Morgana left the beach behind her and headed north-east. A light sea breeze pushed her forward as she flew low behind the woods. Her attack would take the people of Carw by complete surprise.

Almost everyone heeded the warnings of Caddoc and Addolgar. Unfortunately, word did not reach three women who had been fishing on the river. They were caught out in the open when the dragon swept into view. She announced her arrival with a frightening roar that spread terror throughout the settlement. One woman fainted when she was ushering her children indoors and had to be dragged inside.

The fisher women dropped their baskets and ran towards their homes. One broke off and hid behind a building. This decision saved her life. The other two kept together and were killed by the dragon's tail. One was struck so hard she crashed onto the roof of one of the round houses.

Morgana banked to the right and crossed the river. She turned and attacked again. This time fire was her weapon. The roof of the meeting house was set alight with a ball of flame. Carw was now deserted. Its occupants cowered inside, fervently hoping their ordeal would soon end. The dragon made a final pass over the settlement, setting fire to one of the family homes. She signalled her departure with a bloodcurdling roar, before heading to the coast.

Sel and Naw were still among the woods when Morgana's first warning reached them. Sel had heard the roar of the dragon before. Whilst it scared him, he knew they were safe if they remained within the trees. Naw did not cope as well. He was visibly shaking and looked to Sel for comfort.

"It will be alright. If we retreat further into the woods, we will be safe from the dragon."

Naw sat down before he fell down. He started to sweat and his breathing was heavy. His face turned the colour of Addolgar's hair. "What about our message to Gleis?"

"Do you want to go out into the open and be burnt to death or killed by an angry dragon's tail?" Naw shook his head. "I think we will rest a while and see what happens."

A little later, they heard a second roar. They then caught sight of Morgana as she headed towards the settlement on the coast. Sel smiled. "I think we should return home. If they still want us to deliver the message, it will be safer tomorrow."

Naw agreed at once. "Tomorrow sounds like a good idea." The two men took their time as they walked back to Carw.

On the coast, they already knew that Morgana had survived. Seith had seen her return to the stack the previous day. She still had a long thread of vine hanging from one leg. The evening meal was a sombre affair. Gleis explained what he would do if he was a dragon and someone had tried to kill him.

"I will tell you what I would do. I would start killing people to make sure they never thought about trying it again. We must expect to come under attack at any time. There will be no hunting party leaving here tomorrow. We must all stay close to the meeting house. If the dragon attacks, get here as quickly as possible."

Mair stood up. Her hair was in its usual state of wilful abandon. "You boys can stay here all day, but I am going fishing as usual. If I am going to be killed by a dragon, I prefer to die with a full stomach."

Vala joined her. "I am also going down to the inlet tomorrow. We need to eat." Several others nodded their approval. Adain thought about an objection, but knew her mother's mind was set.

Reluctantly, Gleis agreed to the fishing trip. "Very well. Travel quickly over the headland. When you have set the fish trap, keep out of sight and speak quietly. You will not be safe until you return here."

Next morning, five souls set out to the inlet. Mair, Vala and Eres led the way. They were fearless and full of gossip. Menw and Ysperin followed at a discreet distance. They both carried a spear, although this seemed to be a token gesture of defiance. Menw could hardly throw a spear. Ysperin's expertise was to extract them from victims of assault.

The short journey to the inlet passed without alarm. Mair did not like to be rushed, despite some choice words from Vala. They worked their way down the narrow path to the bottom of the cliffs and waited. When the tide was right, they set the fish trap and scrambled over the rocks to the base of the cliff. Here they sheltered from the sun and the attention of Morgana.

Time passed slowly as they waited for the tide to retreat. The five talked as they waited. Their voices were lost among the sounds of the sea. Eventually, it was time to clamber down into the inlet. Ysperin went first. Willow baskets and fish cradles were handed down to him. Vala, Menw and Eres also made their way into the inlet, with help from Ysperin below. Mair remained above, shouting useless advice. Everyone told her to speak more quietly.

The four walked down the sandy inlet towards the fish trap. Baskets and cradles were divided among them. There was very little sea water their side of the trap. The backs of fish could be seen as they jostled to find their way through the barrier. The lattice held firm. The four waded side by side towards the fish. They scooped them up and filled the baskets. This was a good day. Flat fish, mackerel and sea bass were in abundance.

Ysperin had carried some spare vines and willow with him. He checked the lattice and made several minor repairs. Ysperin and Menw then lifted the lattice. Mair was above the inlet on the rocks. Her job was to secure the lattice with vines until it was time to lower it again for the next catch of fish. In time, the five made their way onto the headland with their prize.

They walked back to the settlement. On the return from the inlet, Mair usually brought up the rear. She carried a small basket of fish. She grumbled and laughed as she made her way home. Ysperin kept her company. He had to struggle with a large basket of fish, a damp cradle and a spear tucked under his arm.

Vala, Menw and Eres had now reached the entrance to the settlement. Morgana spotted the two laggards on the headland and swung in behind them. Some of the settlers witnessed the impending attack from the earthworks. They screamed a warning before rushing to the meeting house. Adain shouted to her mother as people crammed to get safely inside.

Mair and Ysperin turned round to face the assault. Morgana's plan was straightforward. She would kill the two with her tail and then set fire to the settlement. Her wings were swept back as she swooped down. Fire rolled out of her nostrils. Her claws instinctively opened. Her tail snaked out behind her, acting as a rudder. In the final moments before the strike, she recognised Ysperin. Something forced her to spare their lives. She roared as she swept over them and the meeting house beyond.

Ysperin told Mair to leave the fish and hurry to the settlement. Mair was traumatised. For once, she could barely speak. She seized the boy's arm. Eventually, she managed to blurt out her thoughts. "I need to return to the sea for a wash. I have had a bit of an accident."

"I think we should try to avoid being killed by the dragon first. We will tidy you up later." Ysperin grabbed her arm and dragged her towards safety. For once, Mair was inclined to hurry.

Morgana turned inland and circled back to the cliffs. She soared down over the defensive ditch and incinerated the roof of the meeting house. Those inside could feel the blast of heat. The turf protected the ceiling and it remained secure. No scorch marks were apparent on the inner lining of animal skins. Those inside trembled with fear as she roared again. Morgana banked to the left and headed back to her lair.

Shortly after, Ysperin and Mair entered the meeting house. Mair smiled. "Something seems to have upset the dragon. I am sorry about the smell. Ysperin was very frightened, but I managed to save him."

Ysperin went bright red. He held his nose and pointed at Mair. She continued to grin amongst all the laughter. Vala stepped forward and gave Mair the briefest of hugs.

Morgana landed gently on her lair. Her claws were now less painful as they found purchase on the warm limestone. She settled down to rest. She would drink tonight and feed tomorrow. The reckoning was far from over.

CHAPTER 22

The Thoughts of a Dragon

You now know many of the physical characteristics of dragons, but what of how they think? The best way to describe what goes on in the mind of a dragon is to imagine a creature that is driven by necessity or instinct.

Having secured a safe place to live, a dragon has just four requirements. It needs a safe place to drink at night. It needs a hunting ground with an ample supply of food. Very occasionally, it is driven by a compulsion to mate. Finally, it seeks to live a peaceful existence, free from the attentions of other dragons. It is not difficult to foresee when problems might arise.

It is perhaps wrong to say that Morgana seeks revenge for Cadwr's attempt on her life. If someone does you an injustice, it is natural to seek some form of redress. It may take time, yet you achieve satisfaction if you are successful. In short, you seek revenge. For dragons, their response is more instinctive. If people stray onto their hunting grounds, they kill them until the threat goes away. If people attempt to kill a dragon, it kills them until the threat goes away. It is a simple response. There is no need for calculation. There is no desire for satisfaction.

Morgana's feelings for Ysperin are more complicated. The boy saved her life when she was most vulnerable. He poses her no threat. She has no need to kill him. Her instinct is to let him live. These are the bare bones of their relationship. The truth, however, is more elusive. A bond certainly exists between them, although it cannot be fully explained.

How does Morgana view the relative threat posed by Carw and the settlement on the coast? So far, Gleis's small settlement has posed little threat. They have left her alone. She liked to listen to their voices as they wafted over the cliffs. Ysperin lived there and he had helped her. In contrast, Carw posed a greater threat. More people lived there. More of their hunters were straying onto her hunting grounds. She knew that Cadwr lived there for a while. Carw was the greater threat and they would command most of her attention.

Morgana's position is clear. She needs to protect her hunting grounds. She also needs to make sure that people do not attempt to kill her. She now has two reasons to kill people. She will keep killing people until she thinks she no longer needs to. Everyone at Carw is in mortal danger. The twenty-five souls on the cliffs are somewhat safer, especially if they stand very close to a boy called Ysperin.

CHAPTER 23
What Next?

When Caddoc and Addolgar entered the meeting hall, it was already full. Apart from one wailing baby, there was total silence. They walked to the front and looked out at the expectant faces. The entire community was seated before them. Caddoc spoke first.

"In a moment, Addolgar is going to speak to you about recent events. I ask you to listen carefully to what he has to say. When he has finished, there will be a chance for you to speak. Please speak freely. We face a great threat and we must all agree on the way forward."

Caddoc nodded to Addolgar before moving aside to join Dera. Addolgar set the scene. He described Cadwr's attempt to kill the dragon. He gave a full account of the steps taken by Olwydd to establish the likely outcome. He then moved on to the crisis they now faced.

"The attempt to kill the dragon has failed. We now face an angry beast that seeks to punish us. Two women from here died today. We must expect further attacks over the next few days. I suggest we reduce the risk of attack in five ways. For the present, stay indoors or close to cover for as long as possible. All hunting on the open ground between Carw and the coast must stop immediately. We need to increase our hunting in wooded areas and open areas north of the river. If we can, we need to catch more fish to maintain our food supply. Finally, we need to use lookouts to give early warning of attacks."

Addolgar waited a while for his message to sink in. He stressed the importance of these five actions. He impressed his audience by repeating them almost word for word.

"Caddoc and I have already talked briefly with the six hunt leaders. We will talk further when this meeting is over. As a community, we have to consider two important questions. If these attacks continue, do we stay here or find a new place to live? If these attacks continue, should we try again to kill the dragon? Let us talk about each of these questions. Firstly, should we stay here or move somewhere safer?"

An elder called Pedw struggled to his feet. He was very frail and his friend Gandwy stood beside him for support. "Until today, most attacks have been on the open ground between here and the coast. We know that the dragon hunts there. We are on his hunting grounds and he has been protecting his food supply. Your plan to stop hunting there makes sense. I agree that we will probably be attacked again because we tried to kill him. I say we follow your advice and see what happens. If he keeps killing us, there will come a time when we will be forced to leave. For now, I say we stay."

Many in the meeting house shouted their approval. Addolgar raised his hand and a dutiful silence followed. "Does anyone think we should make plans now to leave Carw?" Everyone looked around at those seated nearest to them. Nobody spoke.

"Caddoc and I agree with you. We have found a good site

by the river and have built homes here. We will only move if we are forced to do so. I now turn to the second question. If we keep being attacked, should we try again to kill the dragon?"

This time Gandwy rose to his feet alone. "The dragon is very angry with us. I say we do nothing more to annoy him. If we do try to kill him, we need to be almost certain of success." There were further shouts of approval.

Addolgar raised his hand. "Does anyone have any other thoughts?"

Neb stood up. "Do you know Cadwr's secret mixture?"

Addolgar smiled. "Yes, I think I do."

Neb smiled back. "And can you tell us what it is?"

Addolgar lost his smile and pondered his reply. "For the present, I do not want people to start trying to kill the dragon with useless traps. This will only make matters worse. I am worried about the children. They would put all our lives at risk if they started to create this mixture. I do not want to keep secrets from you, but this is one secret that is best left untold."

Neb laughed. "That makes sense. Whatever you do, don't tell Anwar and Eoin."

The tree climbers looked aggrieved. Eoin pushed his way to the front. "I told that fat man his boulder and vines would not work. Don't worry. Anwar and I will kill the dragon. We just need to come up with a bit of a plan."

When the laughter died down, Addolgar spoke again. "Eoin makes a very good point. Some of you may have a good idea of how to kill the dragon. Discuss this with your friends. If they think your plan will work, please speak to me. Caddoc and I are agreed upon this. You must not try to kill the dragon without our approval."

Addolgar raised his hand and swept it over the heads of all

those present. He spoke in the sternest of voices. "You are forbidden from trying to kill the dragon without the approval of Caddoc and myself. Is that clearly understood?"

Around a hundred heads nodded in reply. "Does anyone else wish to speak?"

With great hesitation, young Tarran rose to her feet. "If Cadwr is dead, there is nobody to look after Patch. Can I keep him? I promise I will look after him."

Her soulful eyes and sweet face were impossible to resist. Addolgar wiped a tear from his eye. His voice trembled in reply. "Yes, you can keep him if you let Caddoc and I use him from time to time."

Tarran grinned broadly and nodded her acceptance. Addolgar now surveyed the rest of his audience. "Good luck to you all. Let us hope the dragon forgives us very soon."

Most now stood up and filed out of the meeting house. Some glanced skyward before quickly making their way home. The hunt leaders remained behind to discuss tactics. Their meeting lasted well into the night.

CHAPTER 24

Atonement

Guilt gnawed away at Caddoc. Unable to bear it any longer, he sought out Addolgar.

"We need to talk again with Gleis. I greatly value your counsel, Addolgar, but this is one visit I must make alone. We will have to travel quickly. I will set out with Sel, Eus and Naw. When we leave the woods, we will head for the forest and stay on its edge for a long way to the west. We will then head back towards the settlement. Hopefully, we will avoid being seen by the dragon. The journey may take most of the day. I want to set out at dawn tomorrow. We will talk with Gleis and return the day after."

In his heart, Addolgar knew Caddoc was right. "I could try to ride Patch," he ventured.

Caddoc laughed. "You are both too valuable. Besides, I think the dragon would see you on horseback from a huge distance. Stay here. If the dragon kills me, you will have to lead the people of Carw."

Preparations were made and the four men set out before the sun rose above the woods. A golden glow eased its way across the settlement. Caddoc carried a spear and a square of yew. The rest each carried two spears. Each had a skin of water and a pouch of dried fruit. Speed and vigilance were the bywords.

They walked at a brisk pace until they reached the edge of the forest. Caddoc urged caution. "From now on, we can be attacked by animals from the forest and the dragon. We will travel about fifty paces from the forest edge. If we see the dragon, head straight for the trees."

They made good time. By mid-morning, they had travelled a good distance to the west. They steered clear of several aurochs and a boar. In the distance, a string of wild horses nervously made their way towards Freshwater Beach. A few wolves slipped back into the forest. Nothing caused them any alarm as they kept the sun behind them.

Another hot day beckoned. Caddoc pointed to a small fold in the landscape. "There may be some shade there. We will rest a while and have a drink."

Rested and refreshed, the four pressed on. The dragon was nowhere to be seen. They made good progress and reached their destination by mid-afternoon. Penn spotted them first and alerted Gleis. He walked out alone to meet them.

Caddoc asked whether they had been attacked. Gleis nodded. "And how many dead?"

Gleis could see that Caddoc was genuinely relieved with his reply. Gleis urged them to quickly make their way to the meeting house. "We have been lucky so far. Let it stay so."

Everyone was seated in the meeting house. Vala offered water to the four guests. Caddoc offered Gleis the square of yew and it was grasped. Caddoc asked if he could address all those present. Gleis nodded and Caddoc began.

He was not as eloquent as Addolgar, but he described recent events as best as he could. He started by telling of

Cadwr's preparations. He then described the outcome of Olwydd's investigation. Next, he gave an account of the dragon's attack on Carw. Finally he outlined the decisions taken at the meeting of the whole settlement.

His audience listened in dutiful silence. "I would like to end by saying sorry. We failed to kill the dragon and now he is very angry. We can expect more attacks." He glanced at Adain in acknowledgement of her warning. "I am glad to hear nobody here has been killed so far. If we can help you, we will do so."

"You can help by leaving us and the dragon alone." There was anger in Adain's voice as she pointed accusingly at Caddoc. The cliff dwellers banged their hands on the floor. Naw looked distinctly frightened.

Caddoc was not used to being spoken to in this manner. Not even Dera dared to cross him in anger. Addolgar had warned him that he might receive a hostile reception. He barely managed to control himself. He waited for the noise to cease. "I know you are angry. I am sorry. If you want us to leave, we will do so now."

Gleis stood up. "You are welcome to stay with us tonight. It is too late to head back to Carw. Besides, we need to talk some more. We cannot change what has passed. We can agree what to do next." Adain was about to speak when her mother stopped her. She tugged her arm and sternly shook her head.

Sel asked if he could speak. Both Caddoc and Gleis were surprised, yet encouraged him to have his say. "Caddoc has told you of our plans to reduce the risk of attack. Have you had any similar thoughts?"

Caddoc was pleased with Sel's intervention. It took some sting out of the discussion. It also meant that Gleis had to take the lead. Caddoc knew his best plan now was to shut up and listen.

Gleis continued. "We have taken a few steps to protect ourselves. I think I should start by describing the attack on our settlement." He gave a summary and then moved on to their latest plans.

"At first, we thought about keeping the roof wet to avoid fire. Sea water would kill the grass on the roof. Drinking water is too precious. We already have to carry water from the lake. This is a dangerous business. We now set out shortly before sunset and return in the dark. We may run into trouble with wolves if we have to do this much longer. Luckily, the roof only had minor damage. We hope the roof will keep us safe.

"Fishing at the inlet continues. When we can, we travel at dawn or dusk. To some extent, we are driven by the tides. We now only send younger people who can travel quickly.

"Mair has been told she cannot meet up with Nesta at Flat Rock. Her journey is too exposed. Please tell Nesta. For the moment, all hunting has stopped. We will live off fish, water and dried fruit until things improve. We are a bit fed up but we are still all alive."

Gleis sat down and Caddoc rose to his feet. "I am glad you have all survived. I hope it remains so. If we can help you, we will."

Adain stood up. "You talked about looking for new hunting grounds. You know where we hunt. Tell your hunters to keep off our lands. We don't want to starve because you failed to kill the dragon." Her words were greeted with more banging and shouts of approval.

"You are right. Addolgar warned me that we must avoid clashes on the hunting grounds. Let us agree the boundaries."

Caddoc picked up the square of yew and used one corner to draw a crude map on the floor. "Here is the coast. Here is your settlement. Here is the forest. Here is Flat Rock and here is the lake where you draw water. Where can we safely hunt?"

Gleis motioned to Caddoc to hand him the square. He drew a straight line from the forest to the coast that ran through Flat Rock. "We rarely hunt to the east of this line. We mostly work near the forest, to the west of this line. If you stay to the east, we will stay to the west."

Caddoc nodded. "We are agreed. If any of our men stray over the line, tell them to speak with me."

Adain smiled and pointed a finger at Caddoc. "If any of your men stray over the line, tell them we will poke them in the right direction."

Caddoc joined their laughter. "My men will stay to the east. You have my word."

CHAPTER 25

From the Tops of the Trees

It was late morning. Anwar and Eoin were returning home after a short spell of tree climbing. They had trotted just under half the distance from the woods to the safety of Carw.

Eoin saw the dragon first as she swept in from behind the woods to the east. She was heading straight for them. Both boys turned and ran as fast as they could towards the woods. Anwar did not look back. He ran faster than Eoin and stretched out a lead of about five paces. Suddenly, Eoin stumbled and fell heavily on the hard ground. Dazed, he got to his feet and started to limp towards safety.

Morgana was now upon him. She sank her claws into his shoulders. She swept him off his feet and climbed sharply to avoid the tops of the trees. The pain in Eoin's shoulders was intense. He squirmed and screamed as she lifted him upward.

Morgana's claws had still not fully healed. In some discomfort, she decided to release him over the trees. Eoin just caught sight of the sun shimmering on the river as he tumbled into the canopy. At first, he smashed through the slender twigs. He now felt a stabbing pain in his groin as he struck a branch. He was sure he was going to die.

He was falling more slowly now as the breaking branches

cushioned his fall. Eventually, he came to rest on a V-shaped branch. The two forks were less than a pace apart where Eoin now lay. His feet dangled over one branch. His head and shoulders jutted out over the other.

Eoin was an experienced tree climber. Although in deep shock and immense pain, his instinct was to avoid panic. He needed to stay still and decide what to do next. Far below him, he could hear Anwar's panicked voice. "Are you dead or alive?"

Eoin groaned in agony. "I'm dead, now go and get some help."

"Shall I go and get your mother?"

"No. She will only shit herself and tell me not to climb trees. Go and get Caddoc or Addolgar or Neb or Alawn. Hurry up. I am badly hurt."

Anwar ran for help. First, he went to the woodsman's workshop. Alawn and Neb set out at once for the woods. Anwar now tried to find Caddoc and Addolgar. Nobody had seen them. Just as he was about to give up and return to his friend, he spotted Addolgar coming out of one of the round houses.

Breathless, Anwar quickly explained the plight of his friend. He then ran ahead as Addolgar struggled to the woods as quickly as he could. Neb and Alawn were already peering upward to where Eoin lay motionless.

Addolgar asked Anwar if he could climb all the way up to his friend. The boy surveyed the scene. "The branches there are very weak. If we are both up there, they would probably break."

"How far up can you safely climb?"

Anwar pointed to a branch that ran out from the trunk, about four paces below Eoin.

"Very well. Climb up there. Tell Eoin to stay still. Tell him help is on its way."

Addolgar walked over to Neb and Alawn. "We will probably have to lower him down. Do we have any long vines?"

Neb nodded. "We cut some about six days ago. He is not very heavy. They should be strong enough to hold him."

"Good. Can you get them here as quickly as possible?" Both men set off.

News of Eoin's ill fortune had spread through the settlement. His parents arrived, anxiously looking upwards. Addolgar explained what had happened and how he was planning to get him down. His mother was furious. "I have told him over and over about climbing trees. I will kill him when he gets down."

Addolgar tried to prepare her for the worst. "He is badly injured. I fear the dragon may have done the job for you. I will try to get your son down safely."

It took some time to cast a vine over a strong branch and then throw one end to Eoin. He then had to wrap the vine around him and tie it securely around his waist. Each slight movement brought enormous pain. The vine was not long enough to reach the ground. Anwar had to attach a second vine with a knot described by Addolgar. All this took time. Eoin continued to groan.

Anwar tried to offer him encouragement. "You are doing fine. How do you feel?"

"My shoulders feel like they have spears in them and I think I may have lost one of my stones."

Anwar could see the blood dripping from under his animal skin. He laughed nervously. "Don't worry. I will have a look for it later."

Eoin swore and groaned again. "That Cadwr told us the dragon would not kill us if we helped him. Nobody told the dragon."

Addolgar checked on the progress of the rescue mission. One end of the vine was tied around the waist of Eoin. The vine was draped over a branch above and the two joined lengths reached the ground, with plenty of length to spare. Neb and Alawn now slowly pulled in the slack.

Addolgar shouted up to Anwar. "Tell Eoin he is now safe. If he falls, Alawn and Neb can easily hold him. If he can, tell him to climb towards the tree trunk."

Slowly, Eoin rolled onto his left side and started to ease his way along the branch. He was in great pain and felt sick. Anwar kept encouraging him. When he reached the trunk, he knew he was going to faint. "I have had it. I can't hold on." He slipped and fell a short distance until the two men took the strain.

Addolgar spoke calmly. "He is safe now. Lower him slowly." They let out the vine and the limp body of Eoin slowly reached the ground. His father undid the vine. He then gently picked him up and carried him home.

Addolgar spoke to Eoin's mother. "I will visit you shortly. Seek out Corsen. She will help you. Rub some honey into his wounds and seal it with clay. I hope we have managed to save him."

By now, Anwar had climbed down from the tree. He leant against the trunk and wept for his friend.

CHAPTER 26

Whither the Weather?

The moon had now danced through full shadow and shine without any sign of rain. The ground was hard and the sun continued to beat down. Menw knew the long spell of hot weather was about to end. He had seen the signs before. Everything pointed to a late summer storm. He warned Gleis.

Menw's forecasts were rarely wrong. "When will it strike?"

Menw replied that there would be heavy rain and probably thunder within two days. "My best guess is we will be sheltering sometime tomorrow afternoon. I will know at dawn."

Gleis smiled. "Now is the perfect time to talk to the children about the weather. Show them the signs. Tell them about the coming of the storm."

Menw considered his audience. Tringad and Caw were far too old. Ysperin was old beyond his years and could predict the weather well enough. Llio and Vaddon were babies. His pupils would be Berth, Braith and Teilo.

Berth was the youngest at seven summers and Teilo was the oldest at nine summers. Berth was a shy girl who rarely strayed far from her mother. In contrast, Braith was a very talkative girl. Teilo was a likeable boy, albeit a little cheeky. Menw knew this was going to be an enjoyable trial of wits. The children sat outside in the shade of the meeting house. Ysperin reluctantly agreed to help Menw with matters of discipline.

Menw stood before them. "Today, we are going to talk about the weather."

Teilo was a secret admirer of Adain and liked to mimic her bold approach to life. He jumped to his feet. "It is hot and sunny. The same as always."

Ysperin told Teilo to sit down and stay quiet. Menw asked Braith if she knew her direction points. She nodded enthusiastically. "So where is north?"

She stood up and pointed towards the forest. She then swept her arm round. "And east is over there. South is there and west is over there."

Teilo jumped to his feet again. "What have the direction points got to do with the weather?"

Menw smiled. "Everything. If you sit down, I will tell you." He now turned his attention to his youngest pupil. "Berth, where does the wind usually come from?"

She covered her mouth with her open fingers. "My mother says it usually comes from the south-west."

"Can you point towards the south-west?"

It was not a tricky question. All children were taught their direction points almost as soon as they could talk. She correctly pointed towards the entrance of the meeting house.

"Very good. Now can someone tell me when it is next going to rain?"

The three children looked at each other. Teilo was confused. "Nobody knows that."

"Why not?"

Teilo was now confused and lost for words. Menw

pointed towards the entrance of the settlement. "Come with me. I want to show you something on the headland. Behave yourselves and don't run over the cliff."

The children filed out behind Ysperin and Menw. Ysperin smiled. "I think I am about to learn something too."

"I hope so. There is much I do not know, but I think I know when it is about to rain."

They walked about thirty paces to the west. The group stood around ten paces from the cliff edge. Menw spoke to Berth. "Can you feel the breeze on your face?"

"Yes."

"Is it the same as usual or a little stronger?"

Berth smiled. "It is a little stronger."

Menw now turned to Braith. "Look out to sea. Is it the same as usual?" Braith remained silent. "Look closely. What do you see?"

"There are waves. The sea was as flat as a lake a few days ago. Now there are waves."

Menw turned to Teilo. "Early this morning, you had a pee on top of the earthworks. What did you see, at this very spot?" The two girls giggled and pushed each other.

Teilo cast his mind back. "There was a load of gulls just standing here."

Menw patted him on the back. "That's right. And where did they fly to?"

"They flew north-east."

Menw now asked them all to look beyond the Lonely Wolf stack. "From the rocks, look right out to where the sea meets the sky. What do you see?"

Braith shouted that the sky was very dark there. It was much darker than the rest of the sky. Menw asked them to look very carefully between the darkness of the sky and the sea. The three stared intently. Intrigued, Ysperin joined them. Finally, Berth broke the silence. "I think I can see something. It looks like a flickering flame."

Ysperin confirmed her sighting. "It's lightning. There is a storm far out to sea."

Menw nodded. "There is a storm out there and it is heading in this direction. The wind has picked up and the sea is starting to roll in. The gulls are warning us. They have headed inland to avoid the worst of the storm. Let us return to where we are safe from the dragon. We will talk a little more about the weather, sat in the shade."

They talked about when the storm would arrive. They talked about the seasons. They talked about what happens when the wind shifts to the north or east. Finally, it was time to bring the lesson to a close. Menw thanked them for their attention. "Watch the weather and learn the signs. If you are not careful, the weather can be the death of you. Take heed."

Next day, Menw and the three children watched the approaching storm. Gradually, the sky filled in with shades of black and grey. Their evening meal was accompanied by lightning, rolls of thunder and the sound of torrential rainfall.

CHAPTER 27
After the Storm

Five days had passed since Eoin's brief encounter with the dragon. Corsen told Addolgar that Eoin would probably make a full recovery if his wounds remained free of poison flaming. Each morning and evening, she gently removed the rabbit skin dressings to apply a fresh layer of honey.

Eoin's fear about his groin injury was well founded. Corsen confided in Addolgar. "When he is a little older, he should still be able to seed a child if he can find a girl who enjoys climbing trees." Eoin hated having to lie down or sit still all day. Corsen was insistent. In a few days' time, he could go for short walks only. He was told it would be some time before he could climb again.

Anwar visited him whenever he could. He spent much of the day acting as one of the lookouts for the hunting parties. There were two groups of lookouts. One oversaw the movement of hunters between the series of woods that stretched from Carw towards Pebble Bay. The other group watched over hunters elsewhere.

At first, the use of lookouts was somewhat haphazard. There was much shouting and waving of arms. Any prey had ample warning of hunters nearby. A set of signals was quickly introduced to improve matters. If a lookout held a lowered spear, it meant that all was well. A spear waved from side to side warned of danger. A spear pointed upwards showed that the dragon was in flight.

Most of the lookouts were children. The rest were elders or young men who were too unfit to hunt. Occasionally, lookouts were situated in tall trees. Most stood on the edge of woods or the forest, scanning the horizon for sightings of the dragon.

Addolgar's advice was closely observed by everyone at Carw. When Morgana headed east and hunted on the coastal plain, she saw no humans. The pain in her claws was gradually easing. To reduce the strain when carrying away her prey, she decided to feed only on small deer. One or two a day were sufficient for her needs.

When she was not hunting or resting, she continued to exert her authority. Daily, she swept over Carw in a show of force. She seemed to be less inclined to kill people. A deaf old man was recently killed when he did not heed the warning shouts of others. Nevertheless, three days without a death by dragon was a step in the right direction.

Terror was now her weapon of choice. She would swoop down at great speed and roar her disapproval. On her return home, Morgana also made a small detour to sweep low over the settlement on the cliffs.

The changes suggested by Addolgar had some unexpected consequences. A girl called Rhan was acting as a lookout when she was attacked and killed. She was stood on the edge of the forest, looking southwards towards the coast. A bear rumbled out of the undergrowth and snatched her before she could escape. Several hunters nearby heard her screams and bravely gave pursuit. They managed to recover most of her badly mutilated body.

Later that evening, the unfortunate girl was cremated. The ceremony followed a time-honoured pattern. A funeral pyre was built near the river. Just before sunset, all the inhabitants of Carw made their way to the site. A torch was lit and handed to the girl's parents. They set alight the kindling at the base of the pyre.

Addolgar stepped forward. "Rhan loved and was loved. We saw her enter this life and now we see her leave. She lives on while we still remember her." With heads bowed, the community then repeated his words. They watched and waited until only embers remained.

Hunting near the edge of the forest also proved hazardous. A hunter from Carw was killed by an auroch on the charge. A sounder of boars also assaulted a small hunting party, causing several serious injuries. Another hunter almost died when a large cat attacked him from behind.

On the river, a new set of traps was slowly being built about two hundred paces upstream from the existing site. The tidal reach extended well beyond both sets of traps. Salmon and sea trout would remain the most common catch of the day.

Caddoc and Addolgar were both concerned about the reduction in kills by the hunting parties. It proved more difficult to hunt in the confined spaces of woodland or the forest. It was also easier for wild animals to ambush the unwary.

They both knew that hunting would become even more difficult when winter finally arrived. In poor weather, most animals retreat deep into the forest. The aurochs tended to stay together in compact herds, making attacks very risky. Deer preferred more open woodland. Unfortunately, hunters of deer often clashed with packs of hungry wolves.

This was the time of year when honey started to be collected. Addolgar encouraged everyone to build up stocks. Honey was essential for preserving food. With care, all manner of fruits could be preserved for over half a year. Fruit and honey were boiled together and then stored in special clay pots. These vessels were then sealed with soft wooden bungs and wax.

CHAPTER 28
Boar Roast

Gleis and Adain were stood on the headland, watching the sun slowly slide into the distant sea. Vala approached them. "I think we need to cheer ourselves up. We have all managed to survive the dragon. What we need now is to have some fun."

Gleis laughed. "That's what I have been telling your daughter."

Vala smiled. "No. I am talking about a boar roast. The children love it. We all love it. We should have one soon while the evenings are long and warm."

Gleis did not like boar hunts. Last year, he had been knocked off his feet by a charging beast. Few people die at boar hunts. Many are carried away with serious injuries. "Why don't we roast a side of auroch? There will be more meat."

Vala sighed. "I like the taste of boar. There is no finer flesh than roast boar. If you are too afraid, I am sure Adain will kill one for me." Both women teased Gleis until he relented.

"Very well. All I ask for is a little peace. If your daughter suddenly becomes a widow, I hope your roast boar chokes you. When do you want this roast?"

"As soon as possible. When you have killed a boar, Menw

and I will roast it."

"We already have plans for tomorrow. We will kill your boar the day after. Is that soon enough?"

Vala nodded. "That will be fine. Thank you." She walked back alone to the settlement. Adain stood next to her man and watched the blood-red sun sink from view. Gleis brooded over the coming battle with an angry boar on the charge.

At first light, Gleis started to prepare for tomorrow's boar hunt. Adain insisted that she be part of the hunt party. "Someone has to be there to look after you and help you to your feet."

Gleis swore and prodded her with an imaginary spear. He shared his plans. "We will take a large group. The three attack hunters will be me, Penn and Seith. You will join the drive hunters of Tringad, Caw, Iolo, Cenn and Naw. Iolo will lead."

"So you want me to look after Tringad and Caw, as well as look after you?"

"Tringad and Caw are young, but they are good at looking after girls." Gleis took a step back for safety's sake.

It was time to inspect the weapon store. Gleis pulled out the three spears used for killing boars. They were much thicker and longer than ordinary spears. These heavy weapons were not built for throwing. Their main purpose was to keep a charging beast at bay. Most spears were tipped with flint. These were armed with bluestones. The heavier stone was less likely to fracture under enormous force.

Gleis ran his fingers over the cold stone. He checked the sharpness of the points and the edging. Next, he checked that the heads were securely bound to the shafts. Finally, he tested the strength of the shafts. Satisfied, he returned the three spears to the store.

That evening, Gleis called together the other eight hunters. "Tomorrow morning, we will set out early for The Thickets. We will try to kill a wild boar. If we succeed, we will celebrate with a good roast."

Gleis described his battle plan and what was expected of the drivers and the attack hunters. He finished by offering six pieces of advice.

"When a boar is about to charge, the hairs on its neck stand up. Look out!

"If you are charged at, do not run away. It will catch you and rip you apart. Keep calm and jump out of the way. When it runs past you, seek cover or spear it.

"Keep well clear of its tusks. They will slice you open.

"When we get the chance to attack, we must all be brave and attack together. Aim for the neck or ribs.

"Keep on spearing it until it is dead. A wounded boar is still a dangerous beast.

"Work together and tell others what is going on."

The Thickets was a well-known landmark. The constant flow of a spring meant that its immediate surroundings were very unlike the rest of the coastal plain. At the source of the spring, there was very little vegetation as it was always being trampled by animals seeking water. Nearby, reeds, rushes and sedge all flourished in the wet habitat. Marsh foxtail spread out towards areas of bramble and gorse. Finally, there were dense clumps of blackthorn that gave the site its name.

This terrain was ideal for wild boar. The blackthorn, bramble and gorse provided cover. They could also move unobserved among the tall grasses. There was water and wet soil where they could happily plough for grubs and tubers. They could feed on sloes and bark. Occasionally, they would

A FIENDISH ROAR

kill small deer or enjoy eating frogs.

The day of the boar hunt had arrived. Adain fed Llio before handing her over to Vala. They set off shortly after sunrise. A large herd of wild horses swept before them, heading towards Freshwater Beach. The early morning sun caught the cloud of dust as it slowly settled.

When they reached The Thickets, the hunting party split into two groups. Gleis, Penn and Seith approached from the east and made their way towards the spring. The three deer drinking there melted away.

To the west, Iolo led his driving team of Tringad, Caw, Cenn, Naw and Adain. The task of the driving team was to force the prey to move towards the attack team. With luck, they could then move forward quickly enough to assist with the kill.

The driving team formed a cordon and started to move forward. As they did so, they shouted and struck the undergrowth with their spears. Faced with such a threat, the initial reaction of wild boar is to retreat and look for cover. Iolo kept his team on the move. Occasionally, they caught sight of a boar as it moved away from them.

Gleis could now hear Iolo's team as it drew near. Tringad was taken unawares when a sow boar ran along a narrow path through the thicket to his left. Luckily, the boar slipped as she tried to escape. Tringad attacked immediately. Before the boar could recover, he thrust his spear into her ribs. Adain and Naw responded to Tringad's shout and both skewered the beast. They shouted for joy as she gasped her final breath.

The attack team heard the cheers and decided to join them. Just as they set off, a huge boar emerged from the long grass. He was about four times the weight of a man. His wiry coat was black and grey. He fixed his small, deep-set eyes on his quarry. The hairs on his neck signalled his intent.

He charged straight at the three men and struck Penn before he could evade the assault. One of his tusks ripped his thigh and knocked him off his feet. Gleis and Seith quickly moved in front of Penn to shield him. Seith shouted for urgent help. The boar turned and charged again.

This time, Gleis and Seith were ready with their spears. Just before impact, both men stepped back to absorb some of the shock. Gleis's spear struck the boar between the eyes. The thick skull withstood the impact and he continued on his path. The sheer force of the blow ripped the bluestone from the shaft of his spear. As the boar surged past, his shoulder knocked Gleis off his feet. He landed face first in the boggy earth.

Seith's spear inflicted more damage. He caught the boar in the shoulder and he screeched in pain as the spear tip tore into his flesh. The boar disappeared into some cover. Iolo's group arrived and helped Gleis and Penn to their feet. Just in time, they heard the rustle of tall grass as he prepared to attack again.

Naw picked up Penn's spear and joined Seith at the front of the group. Gleis still held his spear, albeit with no stone tip. Gleis motioned to the others to ready themselves for the attack. Adain, Tringad and Caw stood to the left. Iolo and Cenn were positioned to the right. Gleis ordered Penn to take cover.

The boar lowered his head and charged at Naw and Seith. The rest of the hunters attacked as the boar rushed past. Cenn timed his thrust to perfection. Through the shaft, he felt the bluestone as it forced its way through the ribs and entered its innards. The boar sank to his knees. After several more lunges, the light left his eyes as he rolled onto his side.

Adain walked across to Gleis and wiped some of the mud

from his face. Wisely, she decided that the time was not right to admonish him for not staying on his feet. Nobody spoke. They stood for some time, just staring at their trophy.

To reduce the weight, the entrails of both boar were stripped out before the journey home. They also hacked off both heads to further lighten the load. As the hunting party moved away, several wolves were already following the scent of blood to its source.

The journey back to the cliffs took quite some time. Adain helped Penn as he limped his way home. The rest struggled under the weight of so much flesh. It would be early autumn before Penn was fit again to join the hunt. He had paid a heavy price to satisfy Vala's wish for a boar roast.

CHAPTER 29
The Deadly Curse

In sun-dappled areas of woodland, there grew an unassuming little shrub called Deadly Curse. It reached less than one pace in height, with small lime-coloured leaves and narrow stems. For most of the year, it looked much like any other small shrub. In mid to late summer, however, it burst into flower. The petals were deep yellow and at its centre was a luscious small black fruit.

The fruit looked very much like elderberry. To the unwary, it looked like a fruit that begged to be eaten. Unfortunately, this fruit had two dire side effects. It was both hallucinogenic and fatal. All children were warned not to eat fruits they did not recognise. Then as now, children did not always do as they were told.

A group of women were foraging in the woods near Carw. They were looking for honeycombs, edible fungi and early crops of elderberry and blackberry. Several elders and children accompanied them as they slowly moved through the undergrowth. Young Ren decided to strike out on his own.

It was Ren's ill fortune to stumble across a small shrub with deep yellow flowers. He knelt down and ate some of the fruit. The deep red juice stained his lips as he unknowingly sealed his fate. He returned to his mother. Seeing the stains around his mouth, she told him not to eat any more berries as it would give him tummy ache.

It was on the short journey back to Carw that Ren's mother noticed that something was amiss. At first, her son started to run around with arms outstretched, like a sea eagle in flight. He tried to climb a tall tree with no low branches. He shouted rude words he had heard Neb utter when he accidentally banged his thumb. He rolled around in the grass, giggling uncontrollably.

His mother was embarrassed and bewildered. Why was her little boy acting so strangely? She shook Ren and told him to behave. More of Neb's vocabulary followed as he waved a little finger at his mother. He made strange noises as he ran round in tight circles. Someone offered to seek out Corsen.

Ren's mood had changed by the time Corsen joined them. He was now seized by panic, clinging tightly to his mother. He screamed that the dragon was about to attack. He then threw himself to the ground as the imaginary beast swept over him. He wrapped his hands around his head and wailed like a new-born child.

Corsen had noticed the fruit stains around his mouth and feared the worst. She had seen two cases of Deadly Curse before. Ren's mother asked Corsen if she knew what was wrong with him.

"I am sorry. I fear your son has eaten fruit from the Deadly Curse."

The effects of eating fruit from this shrub were well known. Suddenly, Ren's behaviour made sense. She remained stoic. "What can we do to save him?"

Corsen wiped away a tear. "There is nothing to be done.

All we can do is wait." She fell silent as she was reluctant to describe the inevitable course of events.

Ren's mother took him home. A messenger was sent to seek out his father and bring him back from the hunt. Corsen asked a young woman to seek out Addolgar. When he arrived, Corsen broke the grim news. Addolgar asked Corsen to describe what was likely to unfold.

"If he has eaten fruit from the Deadly Curse, he will act strangely until after noon. He will seem to improve, but start to complain of tummy ache. This will get much worse. He will be in agony by nightfall. He will be dead before dawn tomorrow."

Addolgar held his head in one hand. "Is there anything we can do?"

Corsen shook her head. "If his fate is certain, we must think about bringing an early end to his suffering."

Addolgar stared into the distance. "I will only speak to his parents when his death looks to be certain."

Alawn and Neb had heard of Ren's plight and were expecting a visit from Addolgar. It was late afternoon when he visited their workshop. He looked tired and for once his face revealed his years.

Alawn asked if the boy was approaching death. Addolgar nodded. "And you want us to end his pain?" Their visitor nodded again.

"Are his parents agreed?"

"Yes. They are agreed."

"When will they bring him?"

"Shortly after nightfall."

Neb swore. "We are supposed to create things here. We are not supposed to shorten life."

Most people in Carw knew that the two men killed people when they were in agony and close to death. People rarely mentioned this gruesome service for the community. They were just glad that it was not they who had to perform such a grisly act. Addolgar thanked the two men and left.

At dusk, Alawn and Neb returned to the workshop. They sat in silence until they heard footsteps and a young boy's groans. No words were exchanged when Ren's mother and father handed over the boy. Sobbing, they held each other as they returned home.

Almost before Ren knew what was happening to him, his pain ebbed away and he was at peace. Just before nightfall the following day, the cremation ceremony followed its familiar path. First Rhan and now Ren. Only the names changed as the final words were uttered.

CHAPTER 30
Dicing With Death

It was late afternoon. Addolgar and Corsen sat near the river, watching a wading bird in the reeds. They waited until it had successfully snatched its prey.

Addolgar asked Corsen to describe everything she knew about the fruit of the Deadly Curse. She wiped her brow and sighed. "No more than you, I'm afraid. If you eat it, you do strange things and then you die."

"I picked several berries this morning. I sliced through the fleshy part of the berry with a fine shard of flint. The centre of the fruit held a small amount of clear liquid. It looked like water and had no smell. Do we know which part of the fruit makes people do strange things? Do we know which part of the fruit kills them? Is it the fleshy part or the liquid or both?"

Corsen laughed. "I hope you washed your hands after dicing with death. Why does it matter? We know it is deadly. The best thing we can do is avoid it."

Addolgar shook his head. "It may be useful to know which part of the fruit causes death."

Corsen laughed again. "Has someone upset you? Who are you planning to kill?"

Addolgar smiled. "Don't worry. I am not planning to kill

anyone. There may come a time when knowing what kills people may be useful. Can you help me?"

She greatly admired her companion and was keen to help. "What do you want me to do?"

"I want you to gather a large number of berries from the Deadly Curse. You must carefully slice the fruit and drain away the liquid. I need two separate pots. One pot must contain the liquid only. The other pot must contain the fleshy part of the fruit with all the liquid taken out. Can you do that?"

"Yes, I should be able to do that. When do you need it?"

"It is not urgent. How long will it take?"

Corsen considered the task before her. "I think it will take two or three days."

"Good. Take care. Wash your hands often and do not put your hands to your mouth."

Corsen grinned. "I like Alawn and Neb, but I don't want you leading me to their workshop at nightfall."

Addolgar smiled. "You are very important to me and everyone here. Be careful." He briefly placed a hand on her shoulder and slowly returned to the settlement.

Alawn and Neb were shaping a roof joist when Addolgar wandered into their workshop. He saw their worried expressions and held up his hand. "Don't worry. I am here to ask if you could build something for me."

Both men looked relieved. Alawn asked what he wanted.

"I want you to build a small cage."

Alawn was intrigued. "And what are you going to put in this cage?"

"Rabbits."

Alawn and Neb took some time to stop laughing. Finally, Alawn asked why he wanted to cage rabbits when there were plenty to be caught in the sandy warrens near the coast.

"I want to feed different things to the rabbits and then see what happens to them."

Neb asked what he was going to feed to them and why. Reluctantly, Addolgar gave an outline of his plans. When he had finished, Neb still looked suspicious. "I still do not understand why you want to know what kills people."

Addolgar was suitably vague. He repeated what he had told Corsen. Both men still looked sceptical but agreed to help. The three men briefly discussed the dimensions of the cage before Addolgar took his leave.

Three days later, two rabbits were inside a newly built cage. They were deliberately given very little to eat or drink. Addolgar was now ready to carry out his tests. He put in a little grass, clover and wild flowers into the cage. On a clay plate, he also presented the fleshy part of some fruit from the Deadly Curse. A bowl of water was also included.

The two rabbits eagerly devoured all the food and drink. Over the next few days, very little of note happened. They did become agitated for a while, but settled down as normal. The mouths of the rabbits also bore the deep reddish stains from the juices within the fleshy part of the fruit.

Addolgar now introduced more food into the cage. This time, he did not include the fruit from the deadly shrub. Instead, he mixed some of the liquid from the centre of the fruit with the water. The clay bowl was pushed into the cage.

Addolgar had no idea how much of the liquid from the Deadly Curse to mix with the water. He decided to add roughly one part to four parts water. He watched the behaviour of the rabbits closely. This time, the results were dramatic. They raced round the cage and banged repeatedly into the wooden frame. Their eyes were full of terror. They fought each other. Both then displayed signs of poisoning.

Their suffering was not prolonged. Addolgar then arranged for both corpses to be burnt. He sought out Corsen and described the course of events. Corsen waited until Addolgar finished his account. "So the fleshy part of the fruit has little effect. It seems that the liquid in the centre of the Deadly Curse is the culprit. It makes people do strange things then kills them." Addolgar nodded.

"How is this useful to us?"

"The liquid from the middle of the fruit is clear and seems to have no smell. Added to water, it causes death. If we wanted a poison, this is our best weapon."

"Do you have any victim in mind?"

"Not as yet. It does us no harm to be prepared. Can you collect some more liquid from the fruit?"

"Yes. The berries will remain on the shrub of the Deadly Curse for another twenty days or so. I will collect about three times as much as we already have. That will be enough to kill half the settlement."

Five days later, all the deadly liquid was sealed in two clay jars. These were then placed in a much larger clay container and this too was sealed. This was then safely stored away from prying hands.

CHAPTER 31

Caddoc's Love and Loss

When Caddoc was born, only about sixty souls lived at Carw. His father was a hunter and it was Caddoc's dream to follow in his footsteps. In his early years, he and his best friend Sloan spent most of the day in the nearby woods. They climbed trees and hunted small prey such as deer, rabbits and wild pigs. They also brought home all manner of birds such as duck, crow, pigeon and geese.

By the time they were around ten summers, both boys were accomplished hunters. When they were not tracking small game, they practised their throwing of spears and stones. They also developed their strength by fighting each other. These fights were generally good natured. Caddoc was the stronger boy, yet he occasionally let his friend beat him.

In time, both boys joined their fathers as members of the hunt. Caddoc and Sloan were fifteen summers old when they helped to kill their first auroch. For several years, their lives were devoted to chasing wild animals and local girls.

Within three moons, two events shaped Caddoc's destiny. The first was the sudden death of Sloan. He fell heavily when an auroch on the charge suddenly changed direction. Before he could get back to his feet, the auroch skewered him with one of his horns and tossed him over his shoulder. His fellow hunters managed to drag Sloan clear and drive off the bull. His wound proved to be fatal.

Stricken with grief, Caddoc sought solace in the arms of a beautiful woman called Dera. Unfortunately, she already had an ardent admirer named Kegan and the two men soon clashed. Dera was not helpful as she desired both men and refused to choose between them. She secretly enjoyed having two suitors who were prepared to fight over her.

This love feud soon spiralled out of control. Caddoc taunted Kegan with a challenge of combat and this was accepted. Normally, quarrels were settled without resorting to weapons. This was no ordinary disagreement and Caddoc insisted on a fight with spears. This challenge was also accepted.

It was at this moment that Addolgar entered Caddoc's life. Addolgar had been living at Carw for about a year when the two men started to come to blows. Addolgar had quickly won widespread respect within the community. Both sets of parents asked Addolgar to intervene in the dispute. A duel was inevitable. They simply wanted nobody to get killed.

Addolgar first visited Dera. He asked her to choose between the two men. She told him she desired both men and could not favour one over the other. Addolgar then visited both men separately. He tried to persuade them to resolve the dispute by unarmed combat. Both men said it was for the other to back down first. Reluctantly, Addolgar agreed to act as referee at the forthcoming battle.

All at Carw remembered the match between Caddoc and Kegan. It took place on an overcast evening near the river. Everyone turned out to watch the fight. Each side of the combat area measured about 20 paces. Sturdy vines were stretched along the ground to display the boundary. Beyond the combat area, another set of vines was hung from posts to act as a barrier for the crowd.

Two similar spears were produced for the duel. As Caddoc had thrown down the challenge, Kegan was allowed to choose his weapon. He did so and both men readied themselves. On Addolgar's signal, they advanced towards each other.

Caddoc was the more adventurous fighter. He nimbly moved forward, testing Kegan's defence with thrusts of his spear. Kegan parried his assault and retreated slowly. He skilfully moved from side to side, taking care to steer clear of the boundary vines.

Caddoc taunted his rival. He told him he could not run forever and soon he would have a spear through his chest. Kegan kept calm and watched his opponent like a hawk. The duel took a long time to reach its conclusion. The sun was sinking behind the woods when Caddoc made his decisive move. He suddenly rushed forward, causing Kegan to stumble as he tried to evade the assault. As Kegan crashed to the ground, his spear fell across his chest. Caddoc was immediately upon him and placed a foot on his opponent's weapon. His spear was now jutting into Kegan's throat.

Addolgar stepped forward and ordered Caddoc not to kill his opponent. Addolgar spoke to Kegan. "You have lost this fight. If Caddoc spares your life, do you swear to leave this place at daylight tomorrow and never return?"

Kegan nodded with some difficulty. Addolgar told him that if he ever returned to Carw, he would be killed. Addolgar then spoke to Caddoc. "No purpose can be served by killing this man. Let him go and claim your prize."

Caddoc called for Dera to step forward. "If I let him go, will you swear to be my woman?" Dera, too, nodded and a relieved Kegan clambered to his feet. At first light the following day, family and friends said their farewells and Kegan was never heard of or seen again.

Caddoc was now more than content. He spent the day with his fellow hunters and spent the night with his woman. Life meandered along for almost a year before Addolgar once again played a hand in his life.

CHAPTER 32
A New Leader

The last leader of Carw died shortly before Addolgar joined the settlement. As his illness took a long time to defeat him, people grew used to sorting out their own problems. When needed, the elders talked through issues and showed a way forward.

On his travels, Addolgar had witnessed the advantage gained by a settlement having a strong leader. As more people settled in Carw, disputes became commonplace. Extra mouths to feed put a strain on food supplies. Property theft was rare as few people had possessions worthy of the crime. Stealing food did take place occasionally, however, when extreme hunger beckoned. A settler had the right to kill a food thief, making the crime a gamble for the desperate or the foolhardy.

There was often friction between 'locals' and newcomers. Outsiders were viewed with suspicion until their trust was fully earned. In his short time at Carw, Addolgar knew of several deaths caused by these tensions. As always, jealousy and deceit also played their vengeful games. People sometimes attacked or killed their lovers or rivals. With few laws and no leader, Carw risked a slide into anarchy. Addolgar decided to take action.

After some reflection, he arranged a meeting with Gandwy and Pedw. These two men were respected elders within the settlement. Addolgar voiced his concerns and suggested that the settlement needed a leader. "We need a strong leader who can exert his authority. Our time has passed, but we can provide valuable guidance. What we need is a strong man who will do what we tell him."

Gandwy laughed the loudest. "Strong men tend to do as they please. I agree we need a leader. Do you have anyone in mind?"

Caddoc was Addolgar's preferred candidate. He wanted the two to believe they had chosen him of their own accord. He merely needed to nudge them in the right direction. "I have a person in mind, but I welcome your counsel. I have not lived here very long. You two must have some ideas."

Several names were mentioned before Pedw suggested Caddoc. Addolgar seized his chance. "Caddoc is a wise suggestion. Nobody would challenge his authority after his fight with Kegan. I also think he would listen to our advice. What do you think, Gandwy?"

The suggestion sat easily with him. "Caddoc would make a good leader. Who did you have in mind?"

"It is of no importance. I agree with your choice of Caddoc. He should be our man."

The three decided they should sound him out. Would he be willing to be leader and how amenable was he to taking advice? Addolgar asked who wanted to talk to Caddoc.

Pedw spoke first. "Addolgar, this was your idea. I say you talk to him." Gandwy nodded and the meeting was over.

After Addolgar had left, Gandwy spoke to his companion.

"Do you realise we have just been outflanked by an outsider?"

Pedw smiled. "Of course. He is right though. We need a leader and Caddoc is probably the best man for the job. I suspect Addolgar will become his chief adviser. He will probably only talk to us out of respect for our age."

"And does that bother you?"

Pedw shook his head. "No. I am old and tired. I will only speak against them if I think we are being ill served." Gandwy agreed with his friend. They sat in silence. Both men tried to imagine the likely success Caddoc would enjoy if he accepted Addolgar's offer.

Caddoc was unable to join the hunt for several days as he had twisted his knee during the slaughter of a boar. He sat on the riverbank, feeling sorry for himself. Addolgar approached and asked if he could speak with him.

They talked for some time. Caddoc had two key reservations. Being young, he doubted his ability to make wise and just rulings. He also feared having to speak in front of the whole settlement.

Addolgar decided to deal with the issue of judgements first. "Nobody will force you to make instant rulings. You can seek advice from others and then take your own decision."

Caddoc was wary of Addolgar's intentions. "And who should I turn to for advice?"

Addolgar smiled. "You should talk to people you like and trust. I suggest you speak to Dera as she is your woman. I also suggest you speak to wise men like Gandwy and Pedw."

"And what about you?"

"That is up to you. If you ask for my help, I swear I will try to help you as much as I can."

Caddoc sensed that his offer was genuine. "I do not think

I can speak with authority in front of many people. There is no way to avoid that."

Addolgar smiled again. "When you are leader, you can choose a spokesman. When you want to speak, you can speak. When you wish to remain silent, you can hand over to another. You are the leader. You are in control."

Caddoc was still not convinced. Addolgar tried another line of attack. "Think back to the day you hunted and killed your first auroch. How did you feel?"

Caddoc laughed. "Don't tell anybody, but I was shaking with fear. My best friend Sloan was with me. We tried to pretend we were not scared, but were fooling nobody. Our fathers stood beside us and helped us through the day. After, they told us how frightened they were on their first kill."

"And when you hunt aurochs now, how do you feel?"

"I am nervous, but I know what I am doing now and I enjoy seeing all that flesh sink to its knees."

"It is the same when speaking to many people. At first, you are scared. In time, it becomes easier as you find your feet. Personally, I would rather stand in front of a crowd of people than an auroch."

Caddoc laughed again. "You seem to have an answer for everything. If I become leader, will you be my spokesman and adviser?"

Addolgar hesitated before replying. "Yes, if you promise to also seek advice from Pedw and Gandwy. They have much to offer."

The matter was settled. Addolgar set in motion his plans and almost before the people of Carw knew it, they had a new leader. Caddoc's first speech at the meeting house was memorable. Before he stepped forward, Dera handed him a long spear used for boar hunts.

"I fear that I was not born to be a natural speaker. In future, Addolgar will do most of my talking for me. Before I make a judgement, I will seek counsel from wise people such as Gandwy, Pedw and Addolgar. I am sure Dera will also have her say. Make no mistake. When I make a decision, it will be carried out."

Caddoc now thumped the end of his spear on the ground. "Is there anyone here who wants to challenge my authority?" His voice echoed around the room. Silence followed.

"I will seek to be just. My word will be the final word. You will accept my rule or challenge me in combat. You will die and then we will carry on as before. Is that clearly understood?"

Silence was now accompanied by much nodding of heads. For over two years, there were few tribulations to exercise Caddoc's rule. His first serious challenge came from a lady called Morgana.

CHAPTER 33
A Cold Wind

Early autumn now swept through Carw, bringing cooler breezes and early morning mists. Fruit and honey gathering continued apace before the trials of winter. Animals, too, were anxious to feed well whilst nature allowed. They prospered from fresh rainfall on the grasslands of the coastal plain.

Each morning, herds of auroch and deer wandered from the forest and headed south-east towards Pebble Bay. The open ground here had less heather. Lush grass lured all manner of hungry animals to this strip of land.

Morgana was also attracted to this feeding area. She only had to make the short trip eastwards from her lair to fly over a bounty of flesh on the hoof. In the past, hunters from Carw headed due south to join the feast. The ban on hunting towards the coast was a serious blow.

Most parties now had to strike out west and hunt on the forest edge. A sighting of Morgana allowed the men to seek shelter within the tree line. When aurochs left the forest, they tended to do so in small herds. In time, they spread out as they grazed their way towards their destination.

The size of the herds at the forest edge made hunting a

risky business. Hunt leaders needed great patience to safeguard the men in their care. A common tactic was to target stragglers at the back of the herd. A latecomer could be set upon in a surprise attack. If a herd turned to defend the assaulted animal, men could melt into the trees and seek refuge.

Lurking near the forest edge was fraught with danger. In the open, the main threats were from aurochs and the local dragon. In the forest, they faced threats from bears, boar, large cats and wolves. Hunting parties often moved along the forest edge in files of two. One side scanned for threats from the south and the sky, whilst the other flank watched for movements in the forest. Hunting had become more dangerous and less productive.

The most successful hunt leader was called Lug. His bravery was beyond question. His weakness was an unwillingness to listen to the advice of others. At dawn one morning, Lug led his men as usual towards the woods where Morgana had dropped Eoin into the tree tops. Normally, they would follow the well-trod path through the open woodland until they reached the forest. This stretched westwards towards Freshwater Beach.

As they approached the tree line, Lug suddenly turned left and headed towards the coast. At first, nobody questioned this manoeuvre. They imagined he would stay near to the trees and then turn west and follow the southern edge of the woods until they reached the forest beyond. At the point where the edge of the woods skirted westward, Lug continued to the south.

One of the hunters asked where they were heading. Lug's reply was curt. "We will try to make use of The Wave."

"It will take us too far south. Caddoc has told us we must

not hunt on the coastal plain."

Lug could not disguise his irritation. "I lead this hunting party. You will do what I tell you. The dragon has not attacked us for some time. We need to kill an auroch today and this is our best chance. Keep quiet and follow me."

Reluctantly, the seven men fell into line behind Lug as he strode towards the coast. About six hundred paces from the woods, they reached the start of The Wave. For the most part, the coastal plain to the south of Carw was reasonably flat. At this point, there was a fold in the landscape. The ridge was only about two paces high and stretched for over two thousand paces.

From a certain angle, this landmark resembled one of the long waves that crashed into the sands at Freshwater Beach. If men kept on the eastward side of the ridge, they could travel unobserved right into the heart of the coastal plain. The prevailing winds also meant that any animals heading south-east from the forest would not pick up their scent.

Lug and his men reached the southern end of the ridge. Keeping low, they moved through an area dense with gorse. Lug signalled for his men to sit. They waited as he found a concealed viewpoint. He was gladdened by the sight of aurochs and deer slowly heading in his direction.

All the men had hunted here before. The plan of attack was straightforward. They would wait until an auroch wandered close to where they were hidden. They would attack by hurling spears into the left side of their quarry. They would then quickly encircle the animal and attempt to thrust a fatal blow to the ribs.

A cow obliged by wandering very close to where they were hid. There were few alarms and their prey was quickly brought to her knees. Lug boasted to his men about his choice of hunting ground. Unknown to him, Morgana was already in flight, moving along the coastline. From afar, she glimpsed their movements and the flashes of light from the tips of several spears. She banked and headed inland.

Lug's team had just started to remove the auroch's hide when Morgana struck. Using low cloud as cover, she gave the men almost no time to evade the attack. Lug saved himself by diving into a narrow gap between two gorse bushes. The hunter stood next to him was the first to die. He was enveloped in a ball of flame and staggered around screaming until a friend put him out of his misery with a thrust of his spear. Lug abandoned his men and quickly crawled to a place of refuge.

The dragon turned sharply and attacked again. Three men made the mistake of attempting to run away. They sprinted through the clusters of gorse, towards the southern end of the ridge. Morgana set the slowest of the trio alight. The other two were killed by the lashing of her tail.

As she turned again, she saw two hunters crouching among the gorse, clutching spears. She decided to break off her attack. She gained height before heading towards Carw. The weak sun behind her struggled to break through the patchy clouds.

Caddoc was not at Carw on that fateful day as he had decided to join one of the hunting parties. He now rarely attended the hunt but wanted to witness the challenges of working on the forest edge. As Caddoc was away, Dera decided to seek out her friend Eyslk.

Eyslk's job was to collect fish from the river. Twice daily, she knelt down on the narrow walkway to lift the traps attached to tall poles. The wooden pontoon stretched about two thirds of the river's width. She used a wooden staff tipped with an antler to snare the loops tied to the traps.

Any fish were removed from the traps and these were then baited again. Her task complete, Eyslk would then slowly make her way along the walkway towards the riverbank. She clutched a handrail with her left hand, whilst she struggled with the basket of fish. At the water's edge, another sloping walkway led to the top of the bank.

Dera waited patiently as her friend drew near. Eyslk saw the dragon first and screamed. When Dera turned round, it was too late. As Morgana soared just over them, her tail knocked both women off their feet. They were both swept about ten paces into the river. Dera died instantly with a broken neck.

Eyslk was a little more fortunate. She was knocked unconscious and her body drifted slowly until it became entangled in the reeds. Morgana killed three more settlers and set alight to one of the round houses. Her message to Carw was abundantly clear. On the way home, she picked up a deer for lunch.

Lug assessed the damage to his hunting party. Four of his men were dead. One was cut from thorns of gorse, but was happy to survive. He and the other two were unharmed. Lug ordered his men to gather up as many spears as they could find. The bodies were left where they lay. The auroch's carcass was also left for the wolves. The four men followed The Wave and hurried back to Carw. All feared the sight of Morgana on her return journey.

At Carw, Addolgar sent Eus to find Caddoc and bear him the grim news. Meanwhile, several settlers dragged Eyslk from the riverside. They were shocked to find her still breathing. Corsen was sent for and she did what she could. In time, her patient coughed up a little of the river and made a full recovery.

Lug's men reached Carw long before Caddoc. On learning of Dera's fate, Lug ran directly home. He knew that time was now his enemy. Lug described events to his woman whilst gathering essentials. He grabbed an extra spear and filled his water skin. He also crammed his food pouch with dried fruit and nuts. He slipped into the pouch two shards of flint for fire making. He briefly held his woman's hand before glancing both ways at the entrance. He set off to the south-east, running at a brisk pace.

Dera's body was recovered from the river. Corsen examined her neck where the fatal blow was struck. She removed some river weed from Dera's mouth and tidied her appearance. Finally, she arranged for her to be borne home.

CHAPTER 34
A Time for Revenge

Addolgar sat in the roundhouse, alongside Dera. He tried to imagine how Caddoc was suffering. Would he be driven by grief or rage? He did not have long to wait before he heard the approach of the hunting party.

Caddoc entered alone. He pulled back the animal skin covering Dera's upper body and gently caressed her face. His eyes were moist when he finally turned to his friend. "Tell me everything that has happened."

Addolgar gave a full account of the day's events. When he had finished, Caddoc asked where Lug was last seen. "When he heard of Dera's death, he rushed home and gathered some provisions. He was last seen running in the direction of Pebble Bay."

Caddoc wiped away a tear. "Tell every hunter you can find to assemble as soon as possible at the meeting house. I will be there shortly. Tell them what you have told me." Addolgar was glad to be outside, with the breeze on his face.

When Caddoc entered the meeting house, eleven men were listening in silence to Addolgar. When he had finished his account, Caddoc stepped forward. "You all know it was forbidden to hunt on the coastal plain. Because Lug acted against my order, four good hunters have been killed. He angered the dragon and he has come here and killed another four people. Lug has caused all this death and grief by his stupidity. Now he must die. We will hunt him down and kill him."

Caddoc turned to Addolgar. "You have travelled widely. Where will Lug head for?"

Addolgar had already given this some thought. "He was last seen heading south-east, so the settlement at Redstone is an obvious place. I don't think he will go there though, as it is too near. He will seek refuge far away from here."

Caddoc agreed. "So where will he go?"

"There are two obvious paths he could take. He could double back and head north past the Bluestone Mountains. From there, he could walk to the coast beyond. The other choice is to head east towards Snake River. If he kept travelling upriver, there are many small settlements along the way."

"And how far is it from here to where the Snake River meets the sea?"

"It is almost two days' walk, so I would say it is at least fifty stretches."

Caddoc thought for a moment. "Lug is a wily hunter and knows he is now the prey. What would be his best plan of escape?"

"If he headed north-east, I don't think we would ever catch him. There are no known settlements there. They are called the Empty Lands for a good reason. There is nothing there, apart from marshland and forest. Finding a man there will be almost impossible."

Caddoc gave a weary sigh. "Very well. We will split into three hunting parties. Mabon and you three men will head north past the Bluestone Mountains." He touched each of Mabon's men on the shoulder.

"Urien will lead you three men to the Snake River and beyond." Again, Caddoc picked out the hunt leader's men. "I will lead the rest of us on the short trip to Redstone. Go home and grab the essentials. You will need food, water, flints, three spears and a weather skin. Meet up on the eastern edge of Carw and set off as soon as you can. I order you to kill Lug."

Urien asked how long they should search for their quarry. "Spend at least four nights on your trail. If you feel there is no chance of catching him, return home."

The hunters were about to leave when Addolgar held up his hand. "Talk to any people you meet on your travels. Ask if they have seen a stranger with a scar on his face and bear's teeth around his neck. If you don't find him, keep talking to people on the way home. You might go past him without knowing it. Good luck."

Provisions were hastily gathered and the hunt was on.

CHAPTER 35
Manhunt

It was around noon when the three hunt parties set out from Carw. Mabon and his men headed to the north. For a short while, Uriel and Caddoc's teams trotted together before following their allotted paths.

Caddoc's frequent absence from the hunt soon took its toll. Short of breath, he slowed to a walking pace. His three fellow hunters chatted behind him as they made their way along the open ground and woodland towards Pebble Bay. Caddoc was in no mood for conversation. He kept grief at bay and allowed revenge to drive him forward. About six hundred paces from the beach, they headed south-east over the cliffs to Redstone.

To the west of Redstone, the coastline was limestone. At an inlet, the grey-green rock gave way to red sandstone and hence the settlement's name. About forty people lived here. They used nature's gift to net sea fish in the narrow bay. The remainder of their flesh came from deer, rabbit and wildfowl. As they approached, Caddoc asked one of the hunters to remain hidden in the woods.

"Watch the open space at the back of the settlement. If Lug is there, he might try to slip away as we enter Redstone. Do not confront him. Run down and tell us. We will soon hunt him down."

The three men entered the settlement. Caddoc's two companions laid down their spears. Caddoc held his in case Lug suddenly made an appearance. An elder stepped forward to greet them. Bran knew Caddoc well and held out his hand.

"Caddoc, you and your men are welcome. What brings you to us?"

Caddoc related the day's events. "We are looking for Lug. When we find him, we will kill him."

Bran offered his condolences. "Sadly, your journey has been in vain. Nobody from Carw has been here for some time. I swear to you he is not here."

Caddoc knew he spoke the truth. They talked for a while about the dragon, hunting and the weather. Finally, they shook hands again and the four men set out for home. They reached Carw well before dusk.

Meanwhile, Urien and his men were making good progress towards Snake River. The path they took was the main route to the east. The few people they met on the trail had not seen a man matching Lug's description. This did not surprise Urien. Surely Lug would have the sense to leave the path as soon as he saw anyone journeying towards him.

A good while before dusk, Urien started preparations for a night in the open. He asked his men to look out for something tasty to eat around the fire. Up ahead, he could see a small escarpment of rock to his left. He pointed it out to his fellow hunters. "We will see if we can find a safe place to spend the night with the rocks behind us."

As they were about to leave the path, one of the men glimpsed several deer standing in the shadows. Despite some tree cover, he chanced his arm and unleashed a spear. It avoided all obstacles and struck a buck in its shoulder. It tried to escape but was quickly killed.

The deer was collected and they struggled up through the trees to the small cliff of limestone. Towards the end of the cliff, there was a hollow in the base of the rock. Four men could easily shelter there from the elements. Urien gave each man a task. One was assigned to skin and gut the deer. One was told to gather kindling and prepare a fire pit. The third man and Urien's task was to 'lay the ground.'

Laying the ground involved the construction of defensive barrier to protect the men during the night. The best materials were fallen branches or large bushes, preferably containing thorns. These were then dragged to form a semi-circle around their resting place. Wild animals would now be unable to launch a surprise attack at night. With the rock face behind them, a glowing fire before them and a ring of timber and thorns around them, four men with spears could easily ward off any threat.

They roasted their deer and chatted away as the darkness closed in around them. The group seemed happy enough, apart from the youngest. He ate in silence and rarely smiled. Urien asked him why he had a face like a wounded bear.

"I don't like the idea of having to kill Lug. I have hunted with him many times and I like him. I don't want to see him dead."

Urien tried to reassure him. "Look, I don't think we will ever find him. We don't even know if he has headed in this direction. If we do find him, we have to do what Caddoc ordered us to do. We three will kill him. All you have to do is stand your ground and draw his attention."

"So how will you kill him?"

Urien grinned. "First, we will try to encircle him. Then we will attack by hurling spears at him. Once he is injured, we will move in for the kill. Don't worry. We will probably never see him again. If we do, he will be dead very quickly and then we can all go home."

The young man was not convinced. He looked sullen as he poked the fire with a long stick. He slept little that night and remained moody as they headed towards the sun rising through the tree line.

By mid-morning, they reached the large settlement near the mouth of Snake River. Nobody had seen Lug. The elders were keen to hear their story. Urien was impatient and keen to move upriver to the next settlement. "We have to keep moving forward. When we return in a few days, I swear we will give you a full account."

Having drawn fresh water from the river, they moved inland, following its meandering course. For the next three days, the hunters set off towards the sun on their right-hand side. At each settlement, the message was the same. There were no sightings of Lug. Late one evening, Urien sat with his men in a meeting house. "Tomorrow we will head west towards home. If we are welcome, we will try to spend our nights at settlements along the way."

At each place they stayed, the routine was the same. They were provided with shelter and a little food. In exchange, they told the story of the dragon and the parts played by Ysperin, Cadwr, Lug and Caddoc. The elders knew they spoke the truth. Although no dragons lived nearby, they had all seen them in flight as they journeyed across the land.

Finally, the four men arrived back at Carw to hear some unexpected news.

CHAPTER 36
Hell's Teeth

At first, Mabon and his team moved quickly as they headed towards the Bluestone Mountains. When they finally stopped for the night, the foothills stood before them. There was little time to prepare a good site. They camped under a tree and roasted several rabbits. Before sleeping, all the men checked that they could quickly climb the tree if they were visited by wolves or a bear during the night. They were undisturbed and set off north just before sunrise.

They were following a well-worn track that skirted the mountains to their left. It was late morning when they met an old woman heading towards them. For some reason, she was dragging a small branch behind her. She grinned as the four men approached.

Mabon smiled. "She looks like a cross between Nesta and that mad woman Mair." His three companions were still laughing when he spoke to her.

"Have you seen a stranger today? We seek a man with a scar on his face."

Her eyes gleamed as she cackled, broke wind and spat in one breath. Luckily, the breeze favoured the hunters. "Yes, he passed me not long ago."

Mabon was unconvinced. "What did this man look like?"

The old woman tried to rise from her stoop, but failed. "He was a stranger. He had a scar on his face."

"Where was the scar?"

Like Mair, her grin was toothless. Slowly, she raised three bent fingers to her face. "It was on his cheek. How did he get that scar? I wager it was a bear."

The four men suddenly took their fellow traveller more seriously. "Why do you think it was a bear that gave him that scar?"

"Because of the bear's teeth hanging around his neck."

The old woman watched as the four quickly disappeared from view. It was not long before they spotted Lug in the distance. His gait was unmistakable. He was walking briskly, with a spear in each hand. Occasionally, he stopped to survey the track behind him. Mabon was now faced with a tricky choice. He asked his men to sit and rest.

"Lug is a good distance in front of us. There is little cover here. If we try to catch up with him, we will soon be spotted and he will run northwards until he can lose us. He is fresh and should be able to stay well ahead if we try to rush him. We have to be patient and choose our time to attack. We will rest for a while and then follow him as best we can."

In time, the four men reached a high point on the eastern edge of the mountains. From here, they could survey the entire peninsula. Wistfully, they looked south to Carw and the sea beyond. They pointed to the river and followed its flow into the haven. They followed the coast to the west until it swung back in a crescent shape to the north-east. Showing impatience, Mabon urged his men forward.

They hiked beyond the Bluestones and headed towards

the sea. As they moved downhill, the heather and peat slowly gave way to more vegetation. At first, there were clutches of gorse and bramble. Below them, the landscape was greener before the path disappeared into open woodland. The trees stretched downwards towards the coast.

They could just make out Lug on the path below. With the sun behind them, Mabon knew it would be almost impossible to be seen against the mountain backdrop. He guessed that Lug would want to reach the woodland well before nightfall. The four men continued their descent. Occasionally, Mabon paused to check Lug's progress.

As soon as Lug entered the woods, Mabon broke into a trot. As they approached the trees, they were glad to return to a walking pace. It was now early evening. Mabon knew that Lug would soon start to seek out food and shelter. He signalled the need for silence and stealth. Cautiously, they entered the tree line, searching for any sign of their quarry. Each man held one spear by their right side, ready for instant dispatch.

They moved slowly through the trees, listening for any sound that might betray Lug's presence. A twig trodden underfoot perhaps, or the beating wings of startled birds? Four pairs of eyes scanned the distance for any sign of movement. All was still. Silently, they moved deeper into the woods. The light was starting to fade when they heard the crack of a stick. More breaks followed. Lug was a short distance ahead, preparing firewood.

Lug was in good spirits. He was confident that he was not being followed. Tomorrow morning he would reach the sea and then travel north-east along the coast for at least five days. He would then seek out a new settlement and build a new life. He had left the path and found a large rock that offered him a little shelter and protection. He had slain a wild pig and had gathered firewood. He would eat well and set out refreshed at first light.

Mabon and his men waited patiently. As darkness started to engulf them, they spotted the flicker of Lug's fire. Mabon could see that the fire was a good distance from the path. With the help of moonlight, they moved silently beyond where Lug had left the path. When they were beyond earshot, Mabon urged his men to make quick progress before the light finally failed. They trotted along the path, peering ahead into the gloom. When they could no longer continue, Mabon sought out a refuge for the night.

They too left the path and found some shelter beside a large fallen tree. There was no time to hunt for food. They built a small fire and ate the remainder of their dried fruit and nuts. All four had their weather skins draped around their shoulders for added warmth against the easterly wind. Mabon outlined his battle plan.

"At first light, we will move quickly northwards down the path to find an ideal site for an ambush. I will give final orders when we have chosen our ground. We will kill Lug. We will then find some food. When we are ready, we will set out for home. If you wake up a little before dawn, wake us all up. We don't want Lug to pass us while we sleep."

A little before dawn, Mabon slowly led his men back to the path. They moved down the gentle incline, in search of their site for an ambush. As the sun began to peer through the trees, they found a place where the path was lined by dense thorn and bramble on both sides. Lug would be hemmed in. He could only move forward or retreat along the path when the attack began. Mabon outlined his plan and the trap was set.

Lug had slept well. He chewed a little cold pork before setting off to the north. The weak sun greeted him as he ventured down the narrow path. Suddenly, Mabon stepped out before him, with his spear raised. "Hello, Lug. Where do you think you are going?"

Lug was just about to turn when he was hit from behind by two spears. He had heard their whistle as they sped towards him. One spear struck him in the small of the back. The other smashed into his right shoulder. The force of the blows knocked him to his knees. The pain slammed through his body, causing him to twitch uncontrollably. By the time he looked up, Mabon was stood before him with a fellow hunter. He could now hear his two assailants coming down the path behind him.

Lug stared at Mabon. He managed a few final words. "Tell Caddoc I am sorry." Mabon said he was sorry too. He thrust his spear deep into Lug's heart. The manhunt was over.

CHAPTER 37
Heavens Above

It was long past sunset. Menw was outside, gazing at the stars. In the meeting house, Adain was bored. She was tired of mediating in a pointless argument between Mair and her mother. She grabbed a weather skin and dragged Gleis outside. They stood alongside the old man, looking upward. Finally, Adain broke the silence.

"Tell me, Menw, what are stars and how do they stay in the sky?"

Menw sighed. "You keep asking me the same questions. There is much I do not know about the stars. I will tell you what I know. Some stars are clearly brighter than other stars. Why is this so? It could be that the brightest stars are nearest to us, but I am not sure. We also know the stars slowly move about the sky. They move around in groups. They do not scatter about as if driven by the winds."

Menw pointed to a group of stars in the northern sky. "Can you see those seven stars up there? They slowly move about, but the individual stars hold their position."

Adain looked confused. "I am not sure what you mean."

Gleis laughed. "I am certain I don't know what you mean."

Menw pondered his explanation. "Imagine I have seven

stones in my hand and I throw them upon the ground. The pattern of the stones may suggest a shape, such as a man or an animal. If you then walk in a circle around the stones, other patterns can be seen. The pattern changes, yet the stones remain in the same place."

Both pupils felt that they should nod their understanding.

Adain decided to tease her tutor. "There is much I do not know about the sun. I will tell you what I know. Let me start with the solstice stones." Gleis sighed and rolled his eyes. Menw was happy to indulge her.

"We have two sets of stones. The summer solstice stones tell us when the sun reaches its most northerly point. This is what we call midsummer. The day is long and the night is short. The next day, the sun moves just a little further south. After just over one hundred and eighty days, the winter stones tell us that the sun has reached its most southerly point. This we call mid-winter. Now the day is short and the night is long. Tell me, Menw, why does the sun slowly move in one direction each day and then suddenly decide to move back the other way?"

Gleis offered a plausible explanation. "I think the sun heads north again because it prefers the longer days and the better weather. I know I do."

Menw laughed gently before speaking to Adain. "You keep asking me this question and I still do not have the answer. Before you ask, I also don't know why the moon shines at night or how it changes shape."

Gleis was happy once more to join the collective display of ignorance. "It's the sea I don't understand. From the cliffs, we can see the edge of the world where the sea meets the sky. What stops the sea from flowing over the edge?"

Menw suggested that perhaps the sea and the land go on forever. Adain asked him what he meant.

"When we look towards the north-east, we can see a horizon. If we walk in a straight line, we will arrive at the horizon. The land continues to stretch towards the north-east. There is now a new horizon. It may be the same when we look at the sea."

Gleis looked sceptical. "Do you believe that?"

"It would help to explain why the sea does not flow over the edge of the world." All three smiled.

Menw pointed upwards once again. "We seem to think that there are only the sun, moon and stars in the sky. There is something else up there and I cannot explain it."

Adain made a fatuous remark about a dragon and gulls that Menw ignored. "I told you that almost all the stars move very little in the night sky. There are several stars that seem to move across the sky. You occasionally see them at first light, lurking on the horizon. They rise higher night after night, as if wandering across the sky. Why do these few stars not behave like all the others?"

Nobody spoke. They gazed in wonder until the cold drove them indoors.

CHAPTER 38
Healing Wounds

Corsen was delighted with Eoin's progress. The claw wounds in his shoulder were almost healed and free of poison flaming. The tear in his groin was also well on the mend. She told her patient that a little light tree climbing should be possible in the next ten days or so. She encouraged him to walk a good distance each day to build up his strength.

It would be some millennia before the term 'dracophobia' was first coined, yet Corsen's patient displayed all the classic symptoms. He refused to stray too far from the settlement. When he was outside, he moved furtively, constantly looking upwards. He spent much of his waking hours in the safety of the workshop shared by Alawn and Neb.

The cause of Eoin's behaviour was clear enough. Corsen told Eoin that he must not allow his life to be ruined by a vengeful dragon. Whilst he had suffered some misfortune, this was no excuse for behaving like a startled rabbit. He needed to show some auroch's horn and get on with his life.

Eoin felt a little unloved. "That's easy for you to say. If you had been snatched up and dropped for dead into the tops of the trees, you would be scared of dragons too."

Corsen smiled. "There is only one dragon and I don't

think even he is strong enough to lift me off the ground." She pointed to her ample frame. "What happened to you was nasty. My advice is to carry a spear with you at all times. If he ever gets close to you again, poke him in the eye and use some of Neb's rude words to send him on his way." She laid a hand on the boy's shoulder. "Do not be devoured by your fears. Dream of climbing trees. When you are a little older, dream of girls and hunting."

Eoin nodded. He snatched a spear and headed off towards the woodsman's workshop. He allowed himself a rueful smile as he instinctively looked upwards. He swore at his imaginary foe and thrust his spear towards the sky. As he entered the workshop, he said hello to Efa and Drem. They were working together on shaping a large plank of wood. Alawn and Neb were struggling to drag out an old piece of timber at the back of the workshop.

Neb's language suggested that the manoeuvre was not going to plan. The three giggled as Alawn and Neb swore at each other, laughing loudly as they failed to complete their task. They decided to have a chat with Eoin when Anwar suddenly burst into the workshop.

"Mabon and his team are back. I was there when they brought the news to Caddoc. They have killed Lug. They caught up with him in woodland beyond the Bluestone Mountains. They ambushed him. Mabon delivered the final blow. They then threw his body into a thorn bush. What do you think of that?"

The five looked at each other in disbelief. Finally, Alawn spoke to Anwar. "What did Caddoc say?"

"I will tell you in a moment. I forgot to say that Mabon removed the bear's teeth from around Lug's neck before they threw him into the thorns. When Mabon had finished his account of the killing, he handed the teeth over to Caddoc. He thanked Mabon and the other three men in turn. He then headed towards the river."

Neb looked confused. "Why did Caddoc do that?"

Anwar grinned knowingly. "I followed him. When he got to the place where Dera and the others were burnt, he dug a deep hole with his spear and buried the bear's teeth. Tell me, why do you think he did that?"

Alawn spoke. "Lug killed Dera and the others by disobeying Caddoc. The burial of the teeth was important to him. It was Caddoc's way of telling them that their deaths have now been avenged."

Caddoc was now sat on the riverbank. He tried to take stock of recent events. Whilst he was pleased that Lug was now dead, this was scant reward for the loss of Dera. Grief and anger still burnt deep within him. His thoughts turned to his new child. How was he going to manage with losing his woman and gaining a daughter?

About sixty days before her death, Dera had given birth to a girl called Rhan. She had insisted on the name, in honour of the young girl recently killed by a bear. Fortunately, Dera was not carrying Rhan with her when she went to meet her friend Eyslk. As it was a hot day, she had left her baby daughter with a friend. Rhan was asleep in the meeting house when Morgana swept overhead.

When Dera died, Corsen asked a woman who had recently lost a young baby to care for Rhan. Caddoc visited his daughter several times a day. Each reunion was a blessing and a curse. He was happy that the child Dera longed for was growing stronger as each day passed. The baby was also a constant reminder of Caddoc's grievous loss.

The passing of time did not ease Caddoc's suffering. He sought out Addolgar and tried to describe his feelings. "When I sent out the hunters, I thought I would feel better if they returned with the news of Lug's death. Now that Mabon has killed him, I am still riven with pain and anger. I now know what has to be done. The dragon killed my woman and the mother of my child. Now the dragon must die. Can you find me another dragon slayer who can avenge Dera's death?"

"There may be a way we can kill the dragon." Addolgar immediately wished he had remained silent.

Caddoc's face lit up. "Tell me how it can be done."

Addolgar needed time to think. He told Caddoc that Corsen's advice was needed. As soon as he had found her, he would outline his plan.

CHAPTER 39

On Manoeuvres

Addolgar was fearful of his meeting with Caddoc. During their short walk, Addolgar unburdened his concerns to Corsen. He hastily tried to recruit her as an ally, urging her to throw cold water on any plan to kill the dragon.

The meeting took place in Caddoc's round house. On entering, Corsen was struck by the eerie silence. Until recently, she was a regular guest at her leader's home as she would visit daily to check on the progress of mother and baby. Dera's laughter no longer echoed around the room. Rhan's wailing now took place elsewhere.

The three sat down facing each other. Addolgar wanted to weaken Caddoc's resolve at the earliest opportunity.

"I have asked Corsen to join us as her knowledge of medicine may be useful. There is a possible way we may be able to kill the dragon. I must warn you that the chances of success are slight. I fear that we may only make matters worse. I have now given this some thought. I believe that your idea is our best line of attack. We should seek out a new dragon slayer."

Caddoc knew that it would take a long time to seek out such a man. Someone would have to travel far to the mountains in the north-east. Even if a man could be found with the requisite skills, why would he want to journey so far just to kill one dragon? Caddoc had little to offer such a person for his services. Also, he was impatient. He would seize any chance to avenge Dera's death.

"We may never see another dragon slayer at Carw. You have an idea of how the dragon can be killed. I want to hear it."

Addolgar knew that Caddoc would keep pressing him until he relented. All he could do now was point out every reason why his plan was doomed to failure and the dire consequences of another unsuccessful attempt.

"Do you remember the young boy called Ren? He died after eating fruit from the Deadly Curse. We have taken a close look at this fruit. At its centre is a clear liquid. We now know that it is the liquid that causes people to act strangely, before killing them. The liquid seems to have no smell. If the poisonous liquid is added to water, we know that rabbits will drink the mixture and it will kill them. Corsen, do you agree with what I have said so far?"

She nodded. "Yes, but killing a rabbit is not the same thing as killing a dragon." Corsen was keen to play her part. She decided to bide her time.

Addolgar continued. "I know Cadwr's secret mixture. It should be possible to lure the dragon to feast upon it. If a large bowl of water is placed nearby, we can add liquid from the Deadly Curse. If the dragon drinks from the bowl, we may be able to poison him."

Caddoc smiled. "Good. Go ahead. You have my permission to poison the dragon."

Addolgar raised both hands. "Sadly, it is not that simple. There are some important things we do not know."

"What don't we know?"

"Well, for a start, we know that dragons have an excellent sense of smell. Cadwr taught us that. We know that he was right because the dragon was lured to the sinkhole by the smell of his secret mixture. Corsen and I could not smell the liquid from the Deadly Curse. A dragon may be able to smell it. They are wary beasts. If the water is not pure, I believe the dragon will refuse to drink."

Corsen decided to join in. "Also, we do not know if the poisonous liquid has any taste. The dragon is bound to be cautious. If he drinks at all, he will probably only take a small sip to start with. If there is a funny taste, he will surely not drink more."

Addolgar rejoined the fray. "We also have no idea how much poison we need to add to the water. If we add too little, the dragon might survive. If we add too much, the taste or smell might frighten him off."

Corsen completed the pincer manoeuvre. "I know if I drink liquid from the Deadly Curse, it will kill me. I have no idea why the poison kills people. As we do not know how it works, we have no idea if it will kill a dragon. He might drink the poisoned water and it may do little more than give him a bout of bad guts."

Caddoc was not persuaded. "Yes, but the water might just kill him. We have to try."

Addolgar now opened up a second front. "When Cadwr came here, he was confident he could kill the dragon. His father had killed many dragons using vines and a rolling rock. Cadwr himself had killed five of them. His plan sounded like the death of the dragon was certain. As we know, somehow he survived."

Corsen now took over. "Our idea to poison the dragon is

riddled with uncertainty. We don't know if the dragon will even attempt to drink the water. He might be able to smell or taste the poison. Even if he does drink it, it might make matters worse."

Addolgar closed the argument. "Above all, we must remember what happened when we failed to kill the dragon. He immediately killed several people here and forced us to stay off his hunting grounds. When Lug disobeyed you, the dragon killed four hunters. He then came here and killed another four people. Thankfully, there have been no more deaths. If we try to slay him again and fail, the result will be dire. He will certainly kill many of us. We will probably be forced from our homes and have to live elsewhere. The weather at present is settled enough, but winter will soon be upon us. My advice is to do nothing until we are sure we can kill the dragon."

Whilst Corsen voiced her agreement, Caddoc remained unconvinced. "We have to kill the dragon. You made me leader. I now order you to poison the dragon. I don't want to hear any more argument. I want you to carry out my command as soon as possible."

Addolgar knew his position was almost lost. He had one last delaying tactic. "Very well. I will do as you say. I suggest we tell Gleis of our plan. They surely deserve the chance to prepare for an attack if we are unsuccessful."

Caddoc agreed. "Send a messenger to the coast immediately. Tomorrow, I will travel to the coast with Sel and Eus. I will tell them of our plans. Make all preparations to kill the dragon."

The battle of minds was over. The two left Caddoc alone with his grief.

CHAPTER 40

Poisoned Chalice

When Addolgar entered the workshop, Alawn and Neb were sat near the fire. Both were fashioning handles for axes. Neb looked up. "Hello, Addolgar. Do you want a new rabbit cage?"

The old man smiled. "No. I want Alawn to produce two large wooden bowls."

Alawn rose to his feet. "How big do you want these bowls to be?"

Addolgar shaped the approximate dimensions with his hands. "About this size. Above all, the bowls must have a firm base. I want them to be very difficult to knock over."

Alawn scratched his head. "The last person who wanted a bowl like this was Cadwr. You are not going to try to kill the dragon again, are you?"

Addolgar's silence caused Neb to sigh. "Auroch's bollocks. Here we go again."

Addolgar asked the two men to say nothing for the present. As the scheme may not go ahead, there was no point in causing unnecessary panic. Alawn asked what the plan was this time. Neb offered a possible tactic. "You are going to feed the dragon with as much of the secret mixture as he can eat and hope he gets so fat he can't get off the ground."

Addolgar smiled again. "It's an unusual plan. If my idea fails, perhaps we can try it."

Alawn looked sullen. "If your idea fails, we might not live long enough to try something else. Are you sure it makes sense to try again?"

"Caddoc has ordered me to attempt to kill the dragon and that is what I intend to do. How long will it take you to make the bowls?"

"Three or four days. Will that be soon enough?"

Addolgar nodded. He thanked the men and left. Alawn walked over to where Efa and Drem were working. "Did you hear any of what Addolgar was saying?"

Both shook their heads. "Good. If you did hear anything, keep it to yourselves."

With Neb's help, Alawn dragged out two large logs from the store at the end of the workshop. The logs were then carried to the area where the two apprentices were sat. Both blocks of wood were about a pace in diameter and a little less in height. He then went to his store of stone circles.

Alawn had six stones of different diameters. Each slab had a small hole at its centre. The depth of the stone was less than the length of his little finger. He picked out one of the stones and motioned for Neb to give him a hand. The stone was placed on top of one of the logs.

Neb went over to his workbench. He returned with two stone hammers and several pieces of antler. He shared these with his friend. Alawn slotted his straight section of antler into the hole at the stone's heart. His gentle tapping marked the log below. Meanwhile, Neb took a sharp bone and dragged it around the edge of the stone, scoring a shallow grove into the wood. The second log received the same treatment.

The two men carefully returned the stone circle. Alawn asked Efa and Drem to stop what they were doing and pay attention. "We are going to make two large bowls from these logs. I want you to each work on your own bowl. This is the centre of the bowl and this circle shows the top of the inner rim. Do you understand?" Both nodded.

Alawn then handed each a measuring pole. "Do not worry about the outside of the bowl or the base. Neb and I will work on this. Your job is to hollow out the inside of the bowl to the depth of your measure. You have done this before. Is there anything you want to ask me?"

Both shook their heads. "Good. Start straight away. When you get tired, give us a shout. Neb and I will work on the outside of the bowl while you take a rest."

The two apprentices gathered their tools and set to work. Efa shouted over to Alawn. "What are these for, anyway?" Alawn could not think of a suitable response. He simply said they were for Addolgar. She wondered why the old man would want such large bowls as she happily chipped away at her log. She could not have imagined that a dragon's scaly neck would soon be pressing on the edge of her handiwork.

Addolgar chose Naw to travel to Gleis's settlement. His companion would be a novice messenger who was keen to prove his worth. The days were growing shorter. The two men could not afford any delays if they were to return safely before nightfall. Addolgar's briefing was short. They set off at a gentle running pace.

Good fortune smiled upon them. They had just passed Flat Rock when they spotted a hunting party. As Naw drew near, he recognised Gleis at the head of the group. His message was brief. "Caddoc wants to visit you tomorrow. He wants to talk about the dragon."

Gleis was vexed. "What do you mean, 'he wants to talk about the dragon'?"

Naw shrugged his shoulders. "I do not know. That is all Addolgar told me to tell you. Will you meet with him?"

Gleis did not hide his irritation. "We are low on food at present. I need to be hunting every day. Tell Caddoc I will meet him at Flat Rock. I will set out at dawn. I will not wait too long for him. We must gain some flesh very soon. After we have talked, we can hunt for the rest of the day."

Naw nodded. "Very well. I will tell Caddoc to meet you at Flat Rock early tomorrow morning."

Next day, Gleis and Adain set out with six fellow hunters. They travelled slowly at first in the half light. The gloom slowly gave way to early morning mist. Unexpectedly, the group came across a large herd of deer. They were tightly packed, seeking warmth from one another. The wind was from the north-west, allowing the hunters to creep low towards them. They made good use of some thorn to remain undetected. Gleis signalled the plan of attack. Everyone would hurl two spears into the herd. Hopefully, several deer would be struck.

As soon as they had released their spears, they ran as fast as they could towards their target. Each carried their third spear to finish off any wounded animals. Most of the deer scattered to the north. Adain led the way. One buck had a spear sticking out of its hind quarters. In great pain, it bellowed as it swayed from side to side. She promptly killed it with a thrust through its ribs. Fellow hunters dealt with other injured deer.

Gleis surveyed the killing ground. Five carcasses lay among the heather. This was already a good day's hunting. Gleis spoke to his team. "Adain, Tringad, Caw and I will now go to Flat Rock to meet with Caddoc. After, we will visit the lake. The rest of you can get all this flesh back home. Iolo, you are in charge. When you have finished, you can join us at the lake or hunt some more. You decide."

Cheered by their success, Gleis and his companions set off to their meeting. Caddoc, Eus and Sel were already there, sat on the rock. After exchanging greetings, Caddoc held out a square of yew and this was grasped by Gleis. Caddoc did not waste time. He gave a brief outline of recent events. The cool wind buffeted them as Gleis, Adain and the two young hunters listened in silence.

"We have killed Lug, yet I am still angry. I cannot find peace until the dragon is dead. Addolgar knows a way to kill him. I have ordered him to kill the dragon as soon as he is ready."

Gleis was surprised that Adain said nothing. She stood beside him, with head bowed. Caddoc answered Gleis's questions about the planned attack. When he had finished, Adain took a step forward. She pointed her spear at Caddoc.

Her voice bristled with anger. "Make sure you attempt this madness far away from our settlement. If the dragon survives and kills any of our people, I swear I will hunt you down and kill you. Go from this place now."

Caddoc's hand tightened around his spear. He glanced at Gleis, seeking his reaction. He stared back, remaining silent. "I will warn you before we attempt to poison the dragon." The three turned and headed for Carw.

Adain promptly started to trot to the west. The other three

followed. They formed a line as they headed towards the lake. In time, the pleasure of running slowly lifted Adain's mood. She fell in between Tringad and Caw. "This may be a day you will remember. We are going to try to find you both a woman."

Tringad could not conceal his delight. In contrast, Caw looked concerned. Adain slapped him on the back. "Don't worry Caw, we will try to find you one that does not bite." Tringad lengthened his stride. Gleis and Adain smiled at each other as the ardent young man showed them his heels.

CHAPTER 41
Beside the Lake

The settlement on the lake lay not too far to the north-west of Gleis's home. He liked to visit every moon or so to meet with Yal. He was the leader of about fifty people who lived and worked at the edge of the lake.

The stretch of water was around three hundred paces long and just over one hundred paces wide. For the most part, it was reasonably shallow. Water levels were maintained by several springs at its northern edge. At the south-westerly tip of the lake, a small stream meandered towards the coast. Most of the lake was edged with reeds. Cuttings were regularly made through the reed beds to allow access for fishing.

At various points around the lake, five pontoons of stone and timber stretched out for around thirty paces. These were useful vantage points for fishing. Wooden dugouts were also used upon the lake.

The settlers here rarely hunted aurochs or wild boar. They ate plenty of fish and rabbit. They trapped waterfowl and occasionally hunted deer if herds happened to stray nearby. There was no friction between Yal and Gleis's men as they rarely met on the same hunting grounds.

Great craft was used in their trapping of wildfowl. A large

lattice of vines was stretched over a muddy beach on the lake where duck and geese loved to feed. The vines were kept a good height above the water by two poles. The opposite edge of the lattice was firmly pinned to the ground. When several birds strayed under the snare, children would tug at ropes tied to the poles. They would then run from cover and gleefully snatch up their prize.

Yal was told of their approach. He stood outside the meeting house and waited for Gleis, Adain and the two youths. As they drew near, he welcomed them with a smile.

"Hello. Come inside out of the wind and have some food and drink."

Yal's woman was called Haf. She brought out dried fish and fruit. Wooden tumblers filled with water mixed with fruit juice were handed out. Refreshed, it was time to enjoy a little gossip. Yal opened proceedings. "We hear you are having a bit of trouble with the dragon."

Gleis smiled. "Well, we try to live in peace with him. Unfortunately, the people at Carw have other ideas. Since they tried to kill him, things have got much worse. We have just heard that Caddoc wants to try to kill him again. We are very angry, but there is nothing we can do to stop him."

Gleis then told Yal everything that had happened since Cadwr's failed attempt. He finished with an account of Adain's threat made earlier in the day to Caddoc. Haf laughed gently. "That was brave. Everyone knows Caddoc is handy with a spear. He beat a love rival to win Dera, bless her bones. Let's hope this man Addolgar is successful in his quest."

Adain sighed. "Yes, I wished I had said nothing. But what is done is done. If it comes to it, I am sure Gleis will fight him on my behalf." Stone faced, Gleis shook his head. Only Adain failed to join in the laughter as she reflected upon her plight.

Gleis now turned to the matter in hand. "Yal, you may be able to help me. These two young men are ready to take a woman. Have you a few young women that might look to Tringad or Caw? Of course, you can ask a favour of me in return."

Yal consulted Haf. "Have we any young women to spare around here?"

Haf thought for a while about suitable partners. "Well, there are two that might look to them. There's Taryn and Wena. Shall I fetch them and their mothers?" Yal nodded and she hurried from the meeting house.

Yal smiled. "Taryn needs a strong man. I am not sure either of you two boys are up to the task."

Tringad jumped to his feet. "I am strong. I am more than a match for any woman. If needs be, I will put her in her place."

Smiling, Yal, Gleis and Adain exchanged glances. It did not take long for Haf to round up the four women and escort them to the meeting house. No introductions were necessary. Taryn led the way. She was like a younger version of Adain. She was tall, strikingly handsome and confident. She dispensed with the pleasantries. "So which of you two want to be my man?"

Caw recoiled in shock. Adain would tease him for the expression on his face for some time to come. Tringad liked what he saw and stood up. "If you might look to me, I might look to you."

She took a good long look at Tringad. He was roughly the same height and weight. He might suffice. She needed to find out whether he could protect her. It seemed an unnecessary trait to seek in a man as she was more than capable of looking after herself. "Do you know how to play Strike?"

Tringad grinned. "Of course. It is a game for children. Why do you ask?"

"You and I are going outside to play Strike. If you fight well, I might look to you. If you do not fight well, I will never be your woman."

Everyone followed Taryn as she headed outside. Yal caught Tringad's arm. "Beware. She will probably thrash you. If you want Taryn to be your woman, you are going to have to try to injure her first. My advice is to show her no mercy."

Yal also had a quick word with Gleis. "If Taryn kills Tringad, I hope we can still be friends." Gleis laughed.

"I am serious. Someone is about to get seriously hurt. I hope your man gives her a good beating. She has injured plenty of my men. I wish him a long life."

All children played Strike. Each child had a stick that was roughly their own height in length. The object of the game was to strike your opponent first. You could hit your foe with the side of the stick on any part of the body. You could also prod your target with the tip, as long as it was no higher than the chest. After all, there was little point in losing an eye for the sake of a game.

Taryn had come prepared. She had two staffs with her. They were about the thickness of her wrist. Made of a hard wood, the weapons were about two paces in length. She threw one across to Tringad. "We are not children. There are no rules. We continue to fight until one of us gives in. Any questions?"

Tringad threw his staff from one hand to the other. "No questions. I just—"

Taryn nimbly moved forward and thrust the tip of her staff towards Tringad's groin. Just in time, he beat away the lunge with his weapon. Adain whispered to Gleis. "This is some love match. They have only just met and they are already trying to kill each other."

It did not take Tringad too long to realise he was in a serious fight. He sensed that he was a little stronger than his opponent. His tactic was to keep her at bay by forcing her to retreat at every opportunity. When she tired, he would try to force home his advantage.

Taryn was frustrated by her suitor's skill. Growing weary, she lost composure and started to swing wildly. Tringad seized his chance. He thrust the end of his staff at her left kneecap, causing her to sink to the ground. She continued to swing her staff as she tried to regain her feet. Catching her off balance, Tringad struck her across the chest. She fell backwards and rolled over as she hit the ground. She lay motionless.

Playing a children's game, Tringad now made a child's error. He walked over to Taryn with the aim of helping her to her feet. As he was about to roll her onto her side, she responded by elbowing him in the face. It was a perfectly executed manoeuvre. Her right elbow caught Tringad unawares across the bridge of his nose.

Onlookers heard the crunch of cartilage and bone as Taryn's blow found its mark. Dazed, he felt the blood pour over his chin. Before he could gather his wits, Taryn was upright and on the offensive. She was not burdened by Tringad's sense of fair play. With some relish, she crashed her staff across the side of his head. His knees buckled and he lay unconscious upon the grass.

Yal knelt down to see if Tringad was still alive. "Taryn, I feel sorry for the man who finally looks to you. Go away."

Taryn looked genuinely concerned for her opponent. She

knelt down beside Yal. "Is he still alive?"

"He is still breathing. He may wake up or he may die. Why did you have to strike him so hard? He came here to meet a woman. He was not expecting to meet his death."

She shrugged her shoulders. "I like him. If he recovers, I will look to him."

"Well, if he is stupid enough to look to you, you can thank that blow to his head. Now go away."

Some water was brought and administered to Tringad. Slowly, the light returned and he rubbed the side of his head. "What happened?"

Adain was now beside him. "You just let yourself get beaten half to death by a girl."

He slowly pieced together the details of his fight. "What of Taryn? Is she badly hurt?"

"She has a sore knee. I think she is too much woman for you."

"Nonsense. I want a strong woman. In time, I think I can sort her out."

Adain laughed. "That may be so. Will you get the chance to live long enough though?"

Tringad started to feel unwell. He felt faint and threw up. "Adain, will you help me to the meeting house? I need to lie down and rest for a while." With Gleis's help, they each put an arm around their shoulders and helped the vanquished warrior inside.

Unnoticed by almost all the onlookers, Caw stood next to Wena during the fight. They spent most of the time glancing at each other and smiling. Few words were exchanged. Wena's mother heeded the signs. When the fight was over, she spoke to Caw. "My daughter is still too young to look to any man. Perhaps you could return here next summer? Both of you can then choose if you wish to look to each other."

Caw was both relieved and ecstatic. "I will wait until next summer." Wena glanced at Caw and nodded with a brief smile that would sustain him throughout the winter to come.

When Tringad was laid down, Yal spoke to Gleis and Adain. "I think Tringad should stay here tonight. If he feels well enough tomorrow, I will bring him safely home. I did warn your young man. I am sorry the way things are."

Adain grinned. "All is not lost. Tringad is taken with Taryn. They may choose to fight some more."

"If they do choose to look to each other, I hope they live with you on the coast. I seek only a peaceful existence."

Gleis placed his hand on Yal's shoulder. "She will be welcome to live with us. Besides, I cannot afford to lose a young hunter."

After Gleis, Adain and Caw had departed, Taryn paid a visit to Tringad. He looked a mess. Shades of blue and black had already started to spread across his face. She handed him some water. "How do you feel?"

"I should be fine by morning. You fought well today."

"As did you. Tringad, I should not have struck you so hard. I am sorry. If you will look to me, I will look to you."

Tringad felt the warmth in her voice. He took her hand. "I will look to you."

Taryn smiled broadly. "Where will we live?"

"Will you come with me tomorrow?" She nodded. "We will live at my settlement. Go and tell your mother."

Next morning, the young couple made the short journey with Yal and several companions. For some strange reason, no children at her new home ever asked Taryn to play Strike.

CHAPTER 42
A View from the Woods

Alawn and Neb were happy enough. Each picked up a bowl and admired the craftsmanship. Neb spoke first. "These may not be the finest bowls we have made, but they are surely good enough for a dragon."

"They may be good enough for a dragon, but are they good enough for Addolgar?"

They did not have long to wait. Efa had brought news of the completed woodwork. The old man now stood in the workshop and he, too, inspected both vessels. He placed a bowl on a workbench and pressed on the rim to test its stability. He smiled at the two men. "These are just what I wanted. They are the right size and difficult to knock over. Thank you."

Alawn was anxious to learn of Addolgar's plans. "So what happens next?"

He was willing to share some details. "We have already chosen a site. It is in the open, yet not too far from some woodland. We want to be able to see what the dragon does when he feeds upon the magic mixture. To begin with, we will also fill one bowl with fresh water. Will the dragon drink from the water bowl? If he does drink, how much of the water will he take?"

Alawn scratched his chin. He was about to speak when Addolgar held up his hand. "One step at a time. If the dragon does not drink the water, our plan has failed. If he does drink, we can make further plans. We must watch and wait."

Neb left Addolgar in no doubt as to his thoughts on the matter. The logic of his argument was swamped by a wave of bad language. The old man shrugged. "Nobody can be certain how events will unfold. Your silence is still needed. We must not alarm our people unless we need to."

Before the sun rose next morning, Addolgar oversaw the preparations being made by six men and two boys. Two men each carried a wooden bowl. Two men carried water skins and the two strongest bore clay pots full of honey laced with sorrel. Eoin and Anwar's job was to watch the dragon's every move from a concealed viewpoint among the trees. All also carried a spear to provide some measure of reassurance.

Olwydd was one of the water carriers. Addolgar had asked him to lead the group. After exchanging greetings, Addolgar checked that he was also carrying a measuring stick and a shard of flint with him. Olwydd reassured the old man. "Don't worry. Everything you asked for will be carried out."

It was Corsen's idea to recruit Eoin for this venture. There was little risk to his safety. His contribution would help him to overcome his fears and allow some opportunity for revenge. At first, he was reluctant to help. Anwar managed to persuade him. "Come on, Eoin. We are tree climbers. I don't want to go on my own. Besides, I like showing you that I am the better climber."

Eoin made a rude gesture. "All right. Just remember that I have not climbed since I almost died. A small, easy tree to watch from is fine by me."

The group of eight set out before sunrise. They wanted to place the wooden bowls and be safely hidden in the trees as soon as possible. If they delayed, they knew that Morgana threatened their very existence. They did not have far to travel. The site chosen was around four hundred paces from one of the woods on the way to Pebble Bay.

Leaves had started to fall from some of the trees. Most of the wood, however, contained evergreens, thus providing plenty of cover. Anwar had selected an ideal viewpoint. A large tree grew alongside a pine. One of its branches had spread out directly behind the pine, offering a concealed seating area. Peering through small gaps in the pine branches and foliage, they had an excellent view of proceedings. The branch was only about three paces from the ground. If the dragon approached, they could quickly swing down from the branch and drop to the ground.

Both bowls were filled. Whilst it took some time to extract the magic mixture from the pots, all went well. Addolgar's instructions were very precise. The bowl containing the water was to be sited nearest the woods. When the dragon landed, Eoin and Anwar were to watch his every move. Was the dragon wary? Did he sniff the water? Did he drink any of the water? When they asked why the water was so important, Addolgar told them that all would become clear soon.

Everything was in place. The early morning mist seeped away from the two bowls sat on the coastal plain. The men retreated to the heart of the wood. Anwar and Eoin sat on their branch, clutching the ends of the weather skins around their shoulders. Their spears lay on the ground below.

Eoin broke the vigil with a quiet whisper. "What do you

think Addolgar is up to?"

"He is hoping the dragon will slip and drown himself in the bowl."

Both boys giggled uncontrollably. They then made matters worse by telling each other to keep quiet. Finally, the two settled down and waited for half the morning. Finally, Eoin motioned to Anwar. "I am getting stiff. I am going to stand on the branch and stretch a bit." Holding on to one of the pine branches in front of him, he tentatively eased his way upright. As he glanced to his left, he glimpsed Morgana sweeping in from the south-west. Eoin immediately sat down and alerted his friend.

Morgana had smelt the lure and could now see the two bowls upon the ground. She was aware there were humans in the nearby wood, yet they posed her no threat. She sensed that a trap may have been laid. Her craving to feed on Cadwr's magic mixture was tempered by the need for caution. She made several passes over the bowls, taking great care to examine the surrounding terrain. There was nothing to be seen, apart from the two vessels. There were definitely no loops of vine upon the ground. Satisfied that there was no threat, she prepared to land about twenty paces from the bowls.

She touched down very softly. Slowly, she swept her head from side to side as she scanned the terrain between her and the bowls. Apart from her prize and the water, she could not smell anything untoward. Taking small steps, she moved forwards whilst staring intently at each spot where her feet were about to tread. Finally, she stood before the two vessels.

Morgana briefly glanced at the bowl of water. She now turned her attention to the honey and sorrel. The tree climbers watched intently as she emptied the bowl. When she had licked up all the contents, she moved across to the water. At first, she warily sniffed the liquid. She then took a sip. The water was clear and fresh. She drank a little more. Suddenly, she leapt upwards and flew to the coast.

The two boys swung down from the branch and grabbed their spears. Shouting, they then ran to the middle of the woods. The six men emerged and Olwydd barked his orders. Two men accompanied their leader as they ran towards the bowls. When they arrived, Olwydd quickly repeated his task with the measuring stick. He stood it in the bowl and used his flint to record the new water level. He then poured the water away. "Right, you two. Grab a bowl and run back to the woods." He took one look skywards before following them to safety.

Back at Carw, Addolgar and Caddoc listened carefully to the accounts given by Eoin, Anwar and Olwydd. Caddoc was happy. "That's good. Now we can try to poison the dragon."

Anwar considered what his leader had said. "So that is what the water bowl is for. You are going to add some poison to the water and hope it kills the dragon." Caddoc nodded.

"What poison do we have that will kill a dragon?"

Addolgar held up his hand. He managed to disguise his annoyance that all secrecy surrounding this venture was now abandoned. "I believe the time has come to tell everyone of our plans to kill the dragon. Their lives will be in danger if we fail. They deserve to know."

Caddoc stood up. "Call everyone to the meeting house at sunset. You can tell them everything."

"There is one more thing to ponder. The dragon only drank a small amount of water. As we suspected, he was very wary of a trap. The day after tomorrow, I suggest we do exactly as we have done today, still using fresh water. Hopefully, the dragon will drink some more. Two days after that, we can attempt to poison him."

Caddoc was anxious to press ahead with using poison straight away. After some argument, Addolgar persuaded him that it was not worth risking failure for the sake of two days. That evening, the people of Carw were told of Addolgar's scheme. There was some dissent, but all knew that Caddoc's mind was set. Two days later, Eoin and Anwar sat on their perch in the woods, waiting again for the dragon to feed and drink.

Addolgar's instincts were good. This time, the dragon approached the fresh water less guardedly. She drank most of the bowl's contents. All preparations were now complete for the second planned attempt upon Morgana's life.

CHAPTER 43

Another Big Day

When Olwydd woke up, one of his first thoughts was of Cadwr. He remembered how happy he was as they made their way to the cliffs on that fateful day. By nature, Olwydd was not blessed with the dragon slayer's confidence. A sense of foreboding weighed heavily upon him as he prepared for what lay ahead. He consoled himself with the knowledge that his life was not in immediate danger. He would be safe in the woods. If the dragon drank the poison and survived its effects, the time to really worry would be nigh.

The previous day, Eus and Sel had travelled to the coast to warn Gleis. In turn, a messenger was sent to Yal at the lake. It was barely light when the eight assembled at the meeting house. Corsen and Addolgar joined them. Each carried a small clay pot containing the clear liquid from the Deadly Curse. Each water carrier was handed a pot. Their spears were entrusted to Eoin and Anwar.

Addolgar spoke to Olwydd. "You know what to do. When the dragon has left, hurry back here. We have no idea how events will unfold. Keep a sharp lookout. Good luck."

For the third time, a well-rehearsed plan was carried out. The only change to the routine was the addition of the poison to the fresh water. It was slowly added as the water was fed into the bowl. The six men retreated to safety. Eoin and Anwar climbed up to their perch and waited.

Both boys were nervous. Eoin whispered first. "What do you think is going to happen?"

Anwar shrugged. "I think the dragon is going to drink the poison. If the dragon dies, our troubles are over. If he survives, we are all going to start looking as miserable as Olwydd."

In time, Morgana swept in from the east. She glided in and landed near to the two bowls. First, she feasted on the honey and sorrel. She now turned her attention to the second bowl. She sniffed its contents. If she detected anything untoward, it made no difference. She drank almost all of the water and poison before setting off on her customary route to the coast.

Addolgar's advice was heeded as the eight ran back to Carw at a brisk pace. Eoin's lack of fitness started to show. Fortunately, fear and encouragement from his friend drove him forward until safety was reached. Back at the meeting house, Olwydd gave a brief summary of events to Caddoc and Addolgar. "What happens now?"

Addolgar sighed. "We wait. Only go outside if you have to. Let's hope the poison kills the dragon."

For a while after drinking Addolgar's brew, Morgana suffered no ill effects. She was blessed with great defences to counter the effects of poisoning. Her gut contained a wealth of acids and antibodies that could see off almost any threat. Indeed, she could eat rancid flesh without as much as a hiccup. She also had a large liver that filtered harmful toxins from her blood.

We have seen the poisonous effects of the Deadly Curse upon humans. For us, it lives up to its name. For Morgana, it was little more than an inconvenience. Whilst her internal organs were called upon to work a little harder, it was no cause for concern. In human terms, the effects were about the same as mild indigestion.

We must not forget that the clear liquid from the Deadly Curse had two potentially dangerous effects. It was both a poison and a hallucinogen. Whilst the poison was no more than an irritant, the effects of the drug were cataclysmic.

At first, she felt hot as her blood pressure increased. Her vision became blurred. She could see little now apart from the broad sweep of the sea, the sky and the ground. Her mouth felt dry and her breathing became shallow. Flight suddenly seemed unnatural as she struggled to stay airborne. Morgana's instinct was to land quickly before she fell out of the sky. She stopped beating her wings and glided in to land. She hit the ground hard about two thousand paces north of her home. A shallow gully lay behind her where she had ploughed through the heather on her belly.

About the same time as Olwydd's group had set out that day, another three hunters had travelled to the west. Their task was to stay close to the forest edge and look out for the dragon. If they saw anything of note, they were to return to Carw immediately. One man climbed a tree for a better view. Although Morgana crashed a good distance from where he clung, he knew that the dragon was in serious trouble. As instructed by Addolgar, the three ran back to Carw as quickly as possible.

Despite her bumpy landing, Morgana was not in bad shape physically. Her mind, however, was now in the grip of the Deadly Curse. All semblance of normality was lost. Why had everything changed? The grass and gorse were now shades of blue. Only shapes remained, their edges shifting as they clashed with fresh colours beyond. The suns, for now there were several, turned green. They glowed in an indigo sky.

She felt total panic for the first time in her life as weird thoughts and emotions swept through her. Nearby, a small thorn tree spoke to her as it stretched its arms to the northeast. The tree mocked Morgana for her weakness as it signposted the way to her birthplace.

The Deadly Curse dredged up memories of her early days. She was now with her mother, stood high upon a mountain. Her mother encouraged Morgana to beat her wings, strengthening muscle and sinew for the rigours ahead. When Morgana was finally ready, her mother led her towards the edge of a cliff. She made sure that her pupil watched her every move. When her mother reached the precipice, she bent her knees and leapt away from the rock. She spread her wings and then rhythmically beat them as she first levelled out and then climbed upwards. She turned and then flew over where the young dragon stood. She called to her. As she lay helpless in the heather, Morgana relived that first leap of faith.

Sounds now became twisted beyond recognition. The screeching of gulls pierced her brain, forcing her to violently shake her head in a vain attempt to quell the pain. Above all, she was deafened by the thumping of her heart as it remorselessly sought to leap from her chest.

Poor Morgana's prospects now looked bleak. She had experienced a bad trip home.

CHAPTER 44
Approach With Caution

Yesterday, Ysperin and Menw had worked late into the evening to flesh the hide of an auroch. As soon as Gleis's hunting party returned, the two set to work with wedges of flint. Their task was to scrape off all the flesh and fat from the skin. If this first stage was not completed promptly, they knew the hide would start to rot.

Today, the next step was to salt and wash the hide. They needed to cleanse it of blood and dirt, using saltwater to preserve the skin. Menw and the boy knew of the imminent plan to poison the dragon. They decided to set out at first light and follow the path to the inlet. They reckoned that they would have plenty of time to soak and scrub the skin before the attempt was made.

Their scheme proceeded without drama and the two returned safely home. Most people were inside the meeting house. Gleis had banned all hunting for the day until the dragon's fate was known.

Taryn watched as they tightly stretched the hide over a wooden frame. The skin would be left to dry for several days before the next stage of the treatment could begin. Ysperin was about to go inside when he caught sight of Morgana. He called across to the old man. "Menw, can you see the dragon? He seems to be struggling. Look, he is coming in to land."

Morgana was some distance away, yet her distress was clear to see. They watched as she crash landed. Menw spoke first. "He must have drunk the poison. I wonder if he is still alive."

Ysperin ran to the wall of the meeting house and grabbed a spear. "I don't know, but I am going to find out."

Taryn urged caution. "If he is still alive, he will probably kill you. If you have any sense, you will stay here and wait." She shouted out to Tringad and Gleis. They stepped outside, demanding to know what was happening.

Menw explained the course of events. Ysperin said he had to go and find out what had happened to the dragon. By now, everyone was stood outside. Menw was pestered to repeat his account.

Eres told Ysperin he could not go. The boy was insistent. She looked to Gleis and he shrugged his shoulders. "We need to know if the dragon is dead. If Ysperin wants to go, I will not stand in his way."

Menw stepped forward. "I will go with him. If the dragon is still alive, he will need protection." Everyone laughed as the old man gave an unconvincing performance as a dragon slayer.

Vala now stepped forward. "Menw, you are almost too old to carry a spear. Stay here where it is safe."

Menw shook his head. "I will be safe with Ysperin. The dragon did not kill him when he removed the spear from his side. I am not afraid. Besides, I have always wanted to see a dragon at close quarters. We won't be long." There was no more discussion. Menw and Ysperin crossed the defensive ditch and headed towards where Morgana now lay.

To the north, the three dragon spotters took little time to run back to Carw. As soon as they had spoken, Caddoc ordered some of his most experienced hunters to join him in a quest to finally kill the troublesome dragon. "We will get there as quickly as we can. Take three spears each. If the dragon is still alive, we will plunge as many spears as we can deep into the beast. Let's go."

It was now around midday. Ysperin knew his companion could not be rushed. They chatted as they slowly made their way inland. Morgana was still alive and the worst effects of the Deadly Curse had now passed. Gradually, she returned to some semblance of normality. Sounds became less harsh. Colours slid back to their traditional hue. Her racing heart slowed to a canter. Morgana's problem now was that she was drained of all energy. She lay in the heather, fighting the invitation to sleep.

When the two arrived, Morgana appeared to be dead. Ysperin told Menw that it was always safest to approach a dragon head on. When they were about five paces away, the boy called out to Morgana. "Hello. It's me, Ysperin. This is my friend, Menw. Are you still alive?"

She recognised his voice and felt unthreatened. She lifted a weighty eyelid and surveyed the scene before her. She stared at the two humans leaning on their spears, staring back. Nothing much happened for a while. Morgana concentrated on her breathing, sucking in air and then blowing it back towards them. They could feel and smell the dragon's breath upon them as they continued to stare in awe. Menw was fascinated by the hairs in her nostrils. First, they were drawn inside her nose and then raced outward, like seaweed in a backwash.

Ysperin stepped forward. He ran his fingers across the scales below her eyes. "It is not safe here. You have to go home." He pointed to the cliffs.

Morgana did not understand and did not care. She needed to rest. She knew she was not airworthy. She had no choice but to wait where she lay. Ysperin continued to talk to the dragon. He told her about the poison. He told her that he wanted her to live. Above all, he told her she had to go home.

Menw seized the opportunity to greatly improve his knowledge of dragon anatomy. First, he paced out Morgana's dimensions, from the tip of her tail to the end of her nose. He examined the scales on her neck. Next, he studied the construction of her wings. When he tapped the edging of her tail with his spear, Morgana involuntarily twitched, almost knocking him off his feet. Laughing, Ysperin told him to stop poking the dragon.

The tranquil scene was abruptly ended when nine men were spotted to the north-east. Ysperin guessed they were less than two thousand paces away and closing fast. Carrying spears, their intent was clear. Ysperin shouted to Menw, pointing to the danger.

Ysperin slipped his hands between the dragon's jaw and the heather. He then tried to force her head towards the threat. She would not shift. The boy tried another approach. He walked about ten paces to her right-hand side. After telling Menw to stand well clear, Ysperin shouted at the top of his voice. Surprised, Morgana swung her head round and gazed in the direction of his outstretched arms. Her vision was now almost fully restored. She too saw Caddoc and his men running towards them.

The imminent threat to Morgana spurred her into action.

Her first task was to shift her body to face the men bearing down upon her. Next, she swished her tail from side to side. This was a warning to Ysperin and Menw to grant her plenty of room to manoeuvre. She tested her ability to breathe fire. With little effort, balls of flame rolled away from her, scorching the heather below. Finally, she took a long look at Caddoc's men before crouching low.

Menw stopped Ysperin from confronting Caddoc. He gently placed his arm around his neck, preventing any movement. "Listen. There is nothing to be done. We must stand well back and see what happens."

Caddoc now saw the dragon lying in the heather. Seeing no movement, he assumed the poison had worked its magic. A cautious leader would have approached on three fronts, splitting his forces into teams of three. Two groups would be assigned to advance on each flank. He and two others would probe for signs of life from the front, whilst keeping their distance.

Caddoc's impatience at seeing the lifeless dragon was a costly mistake. The nine men had slowed and walked confidently towards their fate. Morgana's hearing was now fully restored. She gauged their approach as they drew ever nearer. When they strayed within her killing zone, she suddenly pushed up from the ground with her arms and opened her eyes. Before they had time to react, Caddoc and those next to him were set alight. Transfixed, the last thing they saw was the ball of flame billowing towards them.

Caddoc and two others bore the brunt of the assault. Their death could not come quickly enough as the three staggered into each other in extreme agony. Their cries would haunt Ysperin and Menw for many moons to come. Two others suffered some fire damage. They busied themselves by trying to extinguish the flames with their hands.

The old man and the boy watched as Morgana ponderously turned her back on her attackers. Using small steps, she shuffled her way into position. One hunter thought she was about to take flight and urged those still fighting fit to attack. This, too, was a mistake. Morgana now whipped her tail from side to side, knocking everyone off their feet. Satisfied that the threat had now passed, she slowly moved back to admire the devastation.

The casualty list was appalling. Three men were in the final stages of death by burning. Two men had died with broken necks. The rest were unconscious, incapacitated by blunt force trauma. What happened next shocked the onlookers. Morgana slowly moved forward. She ignored the two corpses and the three charred bodies. One by one, she stamped on the heads of the remaining four. Menw later likened the dragon's footwork to a panicked child who had accidentally trodden on an ant's nest. They could hear the sickening crunch as their skulls imploded under the force of the blows.

Menw motioned to Ysperin. "We have seen enough. It is time to go home."

Ysperin was reluctant to leave. "What about the dragon?"

Menw smiled. "I think the dragon can look after himself, don't you? Let's go home. We have a story to tell."

CHAPTER 45
Crying Wolf

When Ysperin and Menw had walked about four hundred paces, they turned to take one last look. Morgana was still on the ground, grazing among the heather and grass. The two set off again towards the cliffs. It had been an unusual day, yet its course still had some distance to run.

They were about halfway home when they saw Morgana fly low over their heads. Surprisingly, she did not head straight for her stack. She climbed towards their home and then turned back towards them. For the first time that day, Menw was fearful. "Ysperin, this does not bode well."

The dragon swooped down and set alight a nearby gorse bush. Unknown to them, three wolves had been lying in wait. Two were incinerated. The third animal managed to leap clear, avoiding the worst of the flames. Howling, it ran off with its hindquarters on fire. In disbelief, they watched the flames turn to smoke as the angry wolf sped across the coastal plain.

They walked a little further. They could now see people stood on the earthworks, looking out for their return. Menw stopped and turned to his companion. His voice was grave. "When we speak of what happened today, we must not mention that you warned the dragon of Caddoc's approach."

Ysperin looked confused. "Why not?"

"Because nine people have just died. The dragon may return to Carw and kill some more. If they ever find out that you helped the dragon, they will want to kill you. They may want to kill us all."

"I have been told to always speak the truth."

Menw put an arm around the boy's shoulder. "That is right. Sometimes, though, the truth is best left unspoken. Promise me that you will never talk about how you helped to warn the dragon."

On their return to the meeting house, everyone was desperate to hear about what had happened. Menw delivered a full account, with one notable omission. When he had finished, Mair struggled to her feet. "Well, I have heard some things in my time, but I have never heard such a pack of lies."

Vala noticed the guilty look on Menw's face as he glanced across to Ysperin. Recovering his composure, the old man confronted Mair. "I have spoken the truth. Why do you accuse me of lying?"

Mair was indignant. "I will tell you why you are lying. For many years, I have walked back and forth from here to Flat Rock. In all that time, I have never ever seen a wolf with his backside on fire."

When the laughter subsided, Vala stood up. "Ysperin, you have remained silent. Do you have anything to say?"

The boy stood up. "No. All of what Menw has said is true."

She sensed that the full story had not been told. When she asked if anything else had happened, Ysperin repeated himself. His inquisitor was still not entirely satisfied, yet decided to let the matter rest.

Gleis now stood up and faced Menw. "Are you certain

that all the men are dead?"

"No. It is possible that one or two still cling to life."

"Did you try to find out if anyone was still alive?"

Menw smiled. "The dragon was stood among the bodies. I did not want to give him the chance to kill two more."

Gleis nodded. "And why did the dragon save your skins by setting the wolves alight?"

"I think the dragon recognised Ysperin as the boy who pulled out the spear from his side. He decided to return the favour."

Adain stood up alongside Gleis. "There is enough light left in the day. We must find out if all the men are dead. Ysperin, will you return with us and show the way? If the dragon returns, we may be safe if you are with us."

Ysperin nodded. Gleis took up Adain's lead. "Iolo and Cenn, grab your spears. We three will set out at once with Ysperin."

Adain handed Llio to her mother. "I am coming too. I am tired of doing nothing all day."

The five set out at a brisk pace. By the time they reached their destination, seven wolves had started to tear flesh from the bodies. Adain squealed with delight as she pointed to one animal whose coat was badly scorched around its rear. Working together, the five efficiently drove off the pack to a safe distance. Sulking, the wolves circled the group, biding their time.

Gleis headed straight for Caddoc. His face was charred beyond recognition, yet his torso was unmistakable. There were no signs of life. Keeping one eye on the wolves, they quickly established that all the men were dead. Gleis said what was already known. "There is nothing to be done here. Let's go home."

Ysperin was shaking. He was deeply shocked at seeing so much death at close range. The stench of burnt flesh turned his stomach. He was also terrified by the wolves slowly skulking around them. He pointed to the threat. "What about the wolves?"

Adain placed a hand upon his shoulder. "See that wolf over there? He is the leader. When I have killed him, the rest will pull back." She took several steps forward. True to her word, she hurled her spear and mortally wounded the large grey. The rest of the pack retreated to a respectful distance.

The five trotted towards the setting sun. The wolves had no reason to follow. They did not have long to wait before their feast could resume in earnest.

CHAPTER 46
False Hope

Morgana recalled the discomfort she had endured on her last landing. She approached the stack with some trepidation. She glided in and then beat her wings at the last moment to halt her descent. Her claws came to rest on the moist limestone and she settled down to a well-earned rest.

Before sleeping, she thought about her immediate needs. Under moonlight, she would travel to the lake near Pebble Bay. Here she would slake her thirst. Tomorrow morning, she would snatch up a deer and feed well before resting during the middle of the day. In the afternoon, she would pay a visit to Carw.

Her last thoughts were of the two settlements. Somehow, the people from the river had caused her to crash and suffer such strange thoughts and experiences. For the second time, the boy from the cliffs had helped to save her life. Today's events had crystallised her feelings towards the humans. The river people had tried to drag her over the cliff. Was it the irresistible food or the water that had affected her so badly today? When she was most vulnerable, they had sent men with spears to try to kill her.

In contrast, the people on the cliffs nearby had tried to

live quietly alongside her. She thought about how weak she was when the boy pulled out the spear from her side. She also knew that she would probably have been killed today if he had not alerted her to the threat from the hunters. All was now clear. The people on the cliffs were her friends. The people from the river were her enemies. They should have left her alone to live in peace. Tomorrow, the river people would be handed another painful lesson.

On the cliffs, nightfall had closed its grip around the meeting house. Inside, most were sat around the fire at its heart. The two youngest, Llio and Vaddon, were already asleep, despite the talk and laughter nearby. Menw and Gleis were deep in conversation. Finally, Gleis briefly spoke to Adain before addressing all those present.

"Today, Caddoc tried to kill the dragon. He is now dead and the dragon lives on. We warned Caddoc, yet he did not listen. I fear for the people at Carw. They are likely to come under attack soon. We need to tell them about what has happened to their nine men. When we have done that, we will tell them to leave the dragon alone." All murmured their approval.

"At first light tomorrow, a small group of us will set out to the lake. When we have told Yal of today's events, we will head north-west towards the forest. We will then turn east and head from Carw. I know this is a long pathway to reach the river. We have no choice but to keep away from the dragon's usual territory for as long as we can. The sun is moving towards the winter solstice. We will not have time to follow this trail and return tomorrow. We will spend the night at Carw and then follow our tracks home. Penn and Seith will journey with me."

Gleis looked for Taryn's face in the dimly lit room.

"Taryn, you, Adain and Tringad can travel with us to the lake. It's a chance to see your parents. Where's Caw?"

Caw stood up. "Caw, do you want to visit the lake? You can spend some time with your girl." Caw nodded with enthusiasm.

Vala stood up. "Can we still fish tomorrow?"

Gleis considered his reply. "If you are willing to spend most of the day there, then I will allow it. Go quickly at first light. Do not attempt to return until late in the afternoon."

Iolo stood up. "What about Cenn, Naw and myself? Can we hunt tomorrow?"

"Only if you hunt to the west. You may try for some goat, but watch the cliff tops. They are very slippery at the moment. Try not to fall to your deaths."

At Carw, everyone was gathered in the meeting house. All fell silent when Addolgar stood before them. He gave a brief outline of the day's events. "Around noon today, Caddoc and eight others left here to try to kill the dragon. As yet, we do not know what has happened. As the sun has gone down, it is very unlikely they will return here tonight."

A woman of one of the dead hunters stepped forward. "So where are they?" Her trembling voice betrayed her deepest fear.

"We will not know until tomorrow. If they managed to kill the dragon, they may have decided to shelter with Gleis on the cliffs. If they tried to return here and ran out of daylight, they may have found shelter in the woods."

Another of the bereaved women stepped forward. Sobbing, she gave voice to the thoughts of many. "And what if the dragon managed to kill them? What will become of us then?"

The meeting house bristled with speculation. Addolgar held up his hand. When silence was restored, he gazed across the sweep of expectant faces. "I am sorry. We have no way of knowing what has happened. We can only wait and see what tomorrow brings."

A few people started to make their way home. Addolgar asked them to pause a moment. "We do not know if the dragon is alive or dead. Gandwy, Pedw and I all believe that hunting should stop until we know more. Stay close to your homes or spend the day here. Try not to worry until we know more."

Eight women endured more than worry that night, torn between hope and despair. All were awake when dawn finally broke. Soon they would learn what had happened to their men.

CHAPTER 47
Save Your Breath

Half the morning had ebbed away before Gleis departed from the lake. The delay was inevitable. He knew that Yal would insist on a full account of yesterday's events. Gossip also took its toll. Finally, they managed to leave the settlement and strike out on their allotted path. Gleis urged his two companions forward. He was impatient to reach Carw as soon as possible.

When they reached the forest edge, they trotted eastwards. Penn and Gleis ran side by side. Penn's duty was to look out for threats from the tree line. Gleis scanned the horizon to his right, seeking any sighting of the dragon. Seith ran just behind them. He was tasked with spotting any threats from the rear.

Apart from one bear and several aurochs straying onto their route, there was little to distract them. They made good time through the light drizzle and lingering mist. The dense forest had now given way to more open woodland. They took the well-trod path into the trees. Gleis slowed to a walking pace.

"We will catch our breath in the safety of the woods. The most dangerous part of our journey is the open stretch before Carw. We may need to make a run for it. Take the chance to have a drink and eat a few nuts."

They chatted until the river and the settlement came into view. With some trepidation, they emerged from the trees. They slowly walked forward about twenty paces. All three searched for any sighting of the dragon. Satisfied that there was no imminent danger, the three ran down the gentle slope to Carw.

With less than a hundred paces to go, Seith pointed his spear to the south-east. "Dragon. Far away on the horizon." Anxiously, Gleis and Penn looked towards the threat. They soon realised they would have enough time to reach safety. They quickened their pace and headed for the meeting house. Morgana was now approaching the woods to the east and closing swiftly.

Tarran decided it was time to check on Patch in the stable nearby. She had just stepped outside when a strange, sweaty man swept her off her feet and tucked her under his arm. Screaming, she was carried inside with two men impatiently following behind. The meeting house was full. Many faces turned to discover the cause of the commotion.

Seith held a firm grip on Tarran's arm. With fire in her eyes, she yelled at the man holding her back. "Let me go. I have to go and look after my horse."

Seith knelt down beside her. "I think you should wait a while. There is an angry dragon out there. You cannot help your horse if you are dead."

The stranger's logic made sense. "You can still let go of my arm." She ran to friends in the meeting house to avoid any further embarrassment.

Addolgar rushed to their side. "Welcome. Do you have news of Caddoc and the others?"

Gleis nodded. "First, you must stop anyone from leaving. We have just seen the dragon heading this way."

Addolgar asked two men nearby to stand guard and warn others of the danger. Hurriedly, he returned to Gleis. "What news do you bring?"

"The worst of all news. Caddoc and his men are all dead, killed by the dragon."

Addolgar was crestfallen. "We thought the poison had brought down the dragon. Are you sure they are all dead?" Gleis nodded.

People had now started to gather around them, demanding answers. Addolgar raised his hands and asked for silence. "We have just been given the worst of news. All the men are dead, killed by the dragon. Please be patient. When I have spoken to Gleis from the cliffs, I will tell you more. Give me time to find out what has happened."

The three strangers and Addolgar found a quiet corner. Gleis repeated the story told by Menw. When he had finished, Addolgar asked one question only. "The boy, Ysperin, did he help the dragon in any way?"

"No. When your men were sighted, the old man and Ysperin stood well back to watch events unfold."

Addolgar asked Gleis if he would address everyone present. Gleis found a good excuse. "These are your people. I think they should hear from you."

Addolgar agreed. "If they have any questions, will you answer them?" Gleis nodded.

In another corner, eight women were consoling each other. Several wept openly. Others were too shocked to display any emotion. Family and friends joined them to offer support.

Addolgar raised his hands once more. When silence was restored, he thanked Gleis and his two companions for risking their lives to deliver the sad news. He then repeated the account given to him. When he had finished, Pedw stepped forward and broke the silence.

"Is this Ysperin the same boy who pulled the spear from the side of the dragon?"

Gleis nodded in reply.

Pedw continued. "There is something strange about this boy and the dragon. The dragon kills nine of our men, yet allows this boy and the old man to watch their deaths. On their way home, he saves their lives by attacking the wolves. Why does he kill us and protect your people?"

Gleis took a deep breath. "We have always tried to live in peace with the dragon. The boy helped the dragon and now the dragon has returned the favour. You have tried to kill the dragon twice and failed twice. I think he is killing you to protect himself."

One of the bereaved women stepped forward. "If this boy Ysperin had not helped the dragon, it would probably have died. Since then, many people from here have died. I say we kill this Ysperin for causing us so much misery."

There was widespread support for this action. Gleis, Seith and Penn feared for their safety as chants for Ysperin's death rang around the meeting house.

Addolgar stepped forward. He waited until all the shouting had ceased. "Killing a defenceless boy is not going to help. Remember, I have spoken to him and I know he has goodness in his heart. All he tried to do was relieve the dragon of his pain. The dragon is our enemy. The people who live on the cliffs are our friends. Let us have no more talk of killing this boy."

Gandwy entered the discussion. "Addolgar is right. We will not ease our grief by killing this boy. I say we have to do two things. Now that Caddoc is dead, we need to choose a new leader. We also have to decide what we are going to do about the dragon. We have lost too many people. We cannot carry on as things stand."

Addolgar spoke. "Thank you, Gandwy. As Gleis has risked his life by bringing the sad news of Caddoc and his men, I think we should ask him for any thoughts he has on the way forward."

Seith knew that Gleis was fearful of speaking in front of a large gathering. Cheekily, he motioned Gleis forward with a grin. Gleis scowled back at him.

"The first thing you have to do is stop trying to kill the dragon. Next, you have to stay as far away from his hunting grounds as possible. Lastly, you have to decide whether you can live with the threat of the dragon nearby. If you cannot, you will have to build a new settlement elsewhere. Whatever you decide, my people will try to help you if we can, as long as you leave the dragon alone."

Silence reigned. Addolgar stepped forward once more. "We need some time to reflect on recent events. I suggest we choose a new leader tonight. The dragon has just flown overhead, so take great care if you venture outside. The fish traps were emptied first thing this morning. We will empty them again later this evening. We have enough food for four or five days, so try not to worry. Good luck to you all."

A little while later, Gleis asked if they could spend the night at Carw. Addolgar smiled. "Yes, but I fear you will have to endure much argument and spoken nonsense."

Gleis laughed. "Have you met Mair at our settlement?"

Shortly after Seith had carried Tarran to safety, Morgana swept through Carw. Nobody was outside. She could hear the voices within the meeting house, yet decided not to waste her breath upon the damp roof. Impatience was not in her nature. She was prepared to wait before seeking retribution.

CHAPTER 48

Follow My Lead

"Do you want to be leader?"

"No. Do you want to be leader?"

"No."

Both men thought back to a time when such an offer would have been cherished. Finally, Gandwy spoke. "So who's your man?"

Pedw did not hesitate. "Right now, we need someone who can lead us out of this mess. For me, the only man clever enough to save us from the dragon is Addolgar."

Gandwy nodded. "The only problem with Addolgar is that he is old and frail. He needs a champion who can sort out any troublemakers."

"I agree. Any suggestions?"

Gandwy smiled. "I have already given it some thought. How about Wod?"

Pedw howled with laughter. "Wod! He is almost as daft as Nesta."

"Yes, but all he has to do is hold a spear and growl at people. Would you argue with him?"

Pedw imagined the tall, thickset Wod prodding him with a spear. "No. So do you want to recruit Addolgar or Wod?"

Gandwy laughed gently. "I will speak to Wod as I know you prefer to speak to someone who makes sense."

Pedw nodded. "So be it. I will speak to Addolgar."

Both men glanced around the meeting house in search of their candidates. Pedw asked Addolgar for a quiet word. As soon as he began his enquiry, Addolgar held up a hand.

"It would be wrong of me to become leader. I have to accept some blame for yesterday's deaths."

Pedw asked for an explanation and this was given. Pedw shook his head. "You may have arranged for the collection of the poison, but it was Caddoc's decision to use it. Corsen told me you tried to persuade Caddoc not to use the poison. Is that true?"

Addolgar nodded.

"Caddoc made the decision that killed him and his men. It was not your fault."

Addolgar shrugged his shoulders. "We chose Caddoc because he was young and strong. Why do you now want a leader who is old and weak?"

"We need a leader who is clever enough to lead us through this crisis. I hate to admit it, but I believe you are the cleverest person in Carw."

Addolgar smiled. "You seem to have forgotten that I cannot defend my authority. If someone challenges me, I would have to stand aside."

Pedw grinned. "If someone challenges you, I suggest you immediately choose a champion. If anyone wants to challenge you as leader, they would have to fight your man."

"And who would be willing to act as my champion?"

"Gandwy and I think Wod is the best man for the job."

Addolgar's surprise was clear to see. "That man scares me

more than any other. Will he do the job and does he even understand what he has to do?"

"Gandwy is talking to him right now. We will know soon enough."

For the rest of his days, Gandwy enjoyed telling Pedw about his conversation with Wod. At first, Wod was reluctant to speak to the old man, as a naughty child might behave when trying to evade a parent. When Gandwy had persuaded him that he had done nothing wrong, the debate began in earnest.

"Wod, I wonder if you could help me."

"Maybe so. Maybe not."

"Wod, we have to choose a new leader tonight. I wonder—"

"No, thank you. I don't want to be the leader."

"No, I think Addolgar would make a good leader. As he is old, he needs to pick a champion. Would you like to be his champion?"

Wod was perplexed. Deep furrows appeared on his thickset brow. "What is a champion?"

"You would have to support and protect Addolgar if anyone wanted to challenge him."

"No, thank you. I enjoy killing aurochs and bears and things. That's what I am good at. I don't want to spend all day looking after an old man."

"You would still be able to hunt. Nobody is likely to challenge Addolgar. If they did, it would be in the meeting house when everyone is here."

Wod considered Gandwy's proposal very slowly. "And what if there was a challenge? Would I have to kill him?"

"Well, yes. But I don't think that will happen."

Wod became agitated. "I don't want to kill anybody. My

mum always told me not to kill anyone. Killing someone is not right. My mum told me that."

Gandwy considered the dilemma. "Well, you would not have to kill him. If you gave the man a good beating and asked him to submit, that would be fine."

Wod grinned broadly. "You mean I could break his leg or something and then Corsen could patch him up."

"Exactly. Do you think you could break someone's leg?"

"As easy as you like. All right. I will be Addolgar's… what was it?"

"Champion."

"That's it. I will be his champion."

Wod was confused by Gandwy's explanation as to how he might become champion later that evening. Gandwy told him not to worry and all would be well.

As the afternoon wore on, small groups gathered to discuss who might become leader. Gandwy and Pedw wandered around, offering encouragement or sowing seeds of doubt. The three strangers stood apart. Gleis warned Seith and Penn to keep quiet during the proceedings later that evening. "This has nothing to do with us. We must say nothing and let them get on with it."

After a little food and drink, the people of Carw were ready to select a new leader.

CHAPTER 49
Decision Time

It was time. Addolgar raised his hand and the task of selecting a new leader began.

"We now have to choose a new leader. Who among you wants to step forward?"

Nobody moved. Wod glanced expectantly towards Gandwy, but thankfully stood his ground. Finally, Pedw raised his hand and Addolgar invited him to speak.

"I do not want to be leader. I want to say something that needs to be said. All of us now face a great threat from the dragon. We need a leader who can guide us through this crisis. We need an experienced leader. We need a clever leader. There is only one man who can help us now and that man is Addolgar." Many shouted their approval.

Addolgar played his part by pretending to be surprised. "Thank you, Pedw. For the last time, is there anyone else who wants to step forward?"

After a long silence, Addolgar raised his hand. "Does anyone object to me becoming leader?" Many heads shook in reply. "So be it. I am now your new leader."

As was the custom, everyone stamped their feet in support. When silence was restored, Addolgar raised his hand once more.

"In the near future, I will have some difficult choices to make. The first thing I want to do is to choose Gandwy, Pedw and Corsen as my advisers. As I am an old man, I also need a champion in case anyone challenges my authority. I choose Wod as my champion."

Murmurs of surprise spread through the assembly.

"If you have something helpful to say, speak to me or one of my three advisers. If you think you can do better than me, speak to Wod."

Most laughed, though the threat was clear enough.

"I support what Gleis said earlier today. All attempts to kill the dragon must end. We must also stay off the dragon's hunting grounds. We have to worry about two things. How can we best avoid coming under attack? Also, can we collect enough food to see us through the winter? Pedw, you have some thoughts on how to avoid attacks, perhaps you can give us your advice?"

The old man cleared his throat. "The dragon is not an early riser. As far as we know, he has never appeared before one hand to the horizon. He hunts in the morning and then returns home. After he has eaten, he takes to the skies again in the afternoon. He always seems to return home again before two hands to the horizon. The message is simple. If you have to go anywhere or do anything outside, do it first thing or just before sunset. The middle of the day is also alright, as long as you are sure the dragon has returned home."

Everyone understood what was meant by one or two hands to the horizon. It was their way of telling the time of the day. Let us imagine it is early morning. Hold out your arm at full stretch and place the lower edge of your palm on the eastern horizon. If the sun has risen above the top of your hand, beware. You have now strayed into dragon time.

Addolgar thanked Pedw. "I have already given much thought to our food supplies. I have spoken to Eyslk and we are agreed that fish traps will be emptied and baited at dawn and dusk. On days when we have seen the dragon return to the cliffs, we will also visit the traps in the middle of the day. Speed is essential. Gossip when you are safely home."

Addolgar paused for a moment. "Before I talk more about our food supplies, I want to say something about what we must do if the dragon attacks. If this happens, it is natural to try to rush to our homes. This is a mistake. You should head for the nearest refuge. Make sure all the children understand this."

The old man held sway over the assembly. Everyone made sure each word was carefully weighed. "Before we move on from fishing, we are also looking into placing a net across the river further upstream. Alawn and Neb are going to see if this is a way of catching more fish."

His delivery was slow and assured. "I now want to talk about hunting. At the end of this meeting, I want to talk to all the hunters. After yesterday and the deaths caused by Lug's actions, we have lost many men. This places a heavy burden on those who remain. We cannot afford to lose more men. We will talk about how to continue our supply of fresh meat as safely as possible. I will ask Gleis and his two companions to join us as I value their experience."

Addolgar paused once more. "We also need to think about eating new types of food."

Gandwy was happy to indulge his new leader. "What do you mean?"

"The people at Redstone eat different food to us. They eat a lot of rabbit and wildfowl. We must eat what is available. There are plenty of geese and duck on the river. We must learn how to catch them. There are plenty of small deer in the woods nearby. We must teach the children how to hunt them. If it is difficult or dangerous to kill aurochs, let us look elsewhere. The important thing is to survive the winter and survive the dragon."

Addolgar sought out Corsen among the sea of faces. "Along the riverbank, there is plenty of bulrush. We already eat some of the green shoots as a vegetable. Did you know the roots and pollen can be ground to make flour? This can be stored very easily. We can also grind the grain from wild cereal. When it is mixed with water and baked, we have another food source. Corsen knows how to make this flour and she will teach us. We will need all the flour we can make when winter comes and food is short."

Gandwy leant forward and whispered to Pedw. "Our leader seems to have made a steady start."

Addolgar was not quite finished. "We will ask several people to visit the lake and Redstone. We must learn new ways of gathering food. Finally, does anyone have anything they want to say?"

Nesta took a step forward. "What about all that lovely sea fish I get from Mair on the cliffs?"

Addolgar smiled. "It is not safe to travel to Flat Rock. I am afraid we will have to survive without your lovely sea fish until the threat from the dragon has passed."

Another old woman shuffled forward. "What if the threat from the dragon continues? Will we have to move away from here?"

"With winter on its way, now is not a good time to move the settlement. I will talk to Alawn and Neb. Before any decision is taken, I need to think about what is involved in such a large task."

Neb swore under his breath. He turned to Alawn. "First, he wants us to build a new fish trap. Now he is thinking of building a new settlement. It looks like you and I are going to be as busy as—"

Neb's woman shot him a disapproving glance. It made no difference. Alawn had a fair idea of what he was about to say.

CHAPTER 50
The Stone Age Diet

Addolgar's ideas quickly bore fruit. The hunt leaders were impressed with the old man's grasp of the challenges facing them. His new hunting strategy made sense and it was readily agreed upon. From now on, aurochs would only be hunted very close to the woods or the forest edge. Large deer such as elk or reds were now the prey of choice. They were also pleased with Gleis's concession on hunting rights. From now on, they were allowed to hunt a further one thousand paces to the west of the line previously agreed with Caddoc.

Just before first light the next day, Olwydd set out with a young woman called Efon towards Redstone. To be safe, they took a long route to their destination. First, they headed eastwards, keeping to woodland whenever possible. Around mid-morning, they walked to the south and then followed the coast back to Redstone. Olwydd carried a spear and a square of yew.

Bran welcomed them and asked why they had come. Olwydd asked if he could start by telling him about all the recent events at Carw. When he had finished his account, the purpose of their visit became clear. "I want to learn as much as I can about how you trap rabbit and wildfowl. Efon wants to learn how you cook what you catch."

About the same time as Olwydd and Efon set out from Carw, Gleis and his fellow hunters headed west. Before noon, they reached the lake. After a long chat with Yal, they trotted towards home. They enjoyed the unseasonably warm breeze being drawn up from the south.

Back at Carw, Dravy was not happy. To be fair, Dravy was never happy, but right now, he was especially unhappy. He was the local butcher. Usually, he spent his time hacking the carcasses of aurochs, deer and the like into manageable chunks of meat. Dravy had a young apprentice called Oled. He learnt how to do what he was told.

Most people steered clear of Dravy. His workplace was on the north-eastern edge of the settlement, allowing the smell of blood and guts to be borne away on the breeze. Hunting parties delivered their bounty to his place of work. They did not linger long. If two hunt parties brought back an auroch on the same day, they were chastised for creating a glut of flesh. In lean times, they were shouted at for being hopeless hunters.

Nothing was ever as it should be in Dravy's world. If Neb was in a charitable mood, he would describe Dravy as a miserable bastard. It was a just assessment. Even Neb's woman would probably have nodded in agreement.

Most people smelt Dravy before they saw him. The stench of his trade clung to him like a tightly wrapped bearskin. His scent and surly disposition meant that his fellow settlers avoided him whenever possible. On the rare occasions that Dravy visited the meeting house, he was encouraged to stand just inside the entrance. Dravy cut a lonely figure. Sadly, no woman had the stomach to take him on.

Luckily, the task of delivering meat to the various

dwellings fell to Oled. The boy proved to be a useful intermediary. Neb made sure that Dravy never had to visit the workshop to demand new tools for cleaving meat. Oled was regularly armed with new weapons to bring to his boss.

The previous evening, Addolgar had asked the people of Carw to consider new sources of food supply. The local children took up the challenge with uncommon zeal. By noon, a steady stream of flesh was being brought to Dravy's place of work. Some of the deliveries were useful, such as small deer, rabbit and the occasional duck. Many of the offerings were unwelcome, such as fox, squirrels and long, thin, furry animals that nobody even knew the name of. If truth be told, much of the produce had been dead for some time.

It did not take much to upset Dravy. Today, he was on the wrong side of apoplectic. He shouted at Oled to go and fetch Addolgar.

"What shall I tell him?" For his own safety, Oled was already heading for the doorway as he waited for his mentor's considered response.

"Tell him I am drowning in useless, putrid flesh and I am going to kill the next ugly child who enters this place."

Young Oled took his time to seek out his new leader. He kept a sharp lookout for the dragon, yet the silence and fresh air made the risk seem worthwhile. His message was brief. "Dravy is in a foul mood and he wants to see you straight away."

Addolgar had witnessed the trail of dead specimens heading towards the butcher. He told Oled he would be there shortly. The boy wore a soulful expression. "Please do not take too long. You may find me carved up into small pieces."

Addolgar decided to let Dravy have a good rant. When he

had finished, the old man asked him what he was prepared to accept. "I will take auroch, bear, deer, goat, rabbit, pig, geese, duck and nothing else. It has to have been alive on the day it is brought to me or else I will throw it in the river. Is that clear enough for you?"

Addolgar patted him on the back. "That is perfectly clear. I will tell everyone at the meeting house tonight. Thank you for all your hard work." Like Oled, the old man was pleased to step out into the fresh air, enjoying his own company.

To keep them busy, Corsen rounded up some of the recently bereaved women and described the task before them. On dry days, they would cut down bulrush at dawn and dusk. This would be stored in the narrow building by the river. The bulrush would be hung and left to dry. When it was time, Corsen would show them how to collect pollen from the heads. She would also demonstrate how to cut up the dry root into small pieces. Finally, she would show them the laborious process of pounding and grinding the pollen and root until a serviceable flour was produced.

Small changes were underway. It seemed they now had the means to feed themselves throughout the rigours of the winter. The main threat on the horizon was the local dragon. Unknown to the people of Carw, the threat was to loom large very soon.

CHAPTER 51
Running Home

At dawn, around twenty children set out most days from Carw to hunt in the nearby woods. Some carried snares to trap rabbits. Most carried spears, in search of small deer such as roe. On the rare occasions when some dangerous predator was sighted, such as a bear, the young hunters withdrew to safer glades.

A small group had spotted some deer at the edge of the wood. Under cover, they tried to encircle their prey. All hunters know the moment deer are about to scatter. They suddenly become very alert and shake their heads, searching for possible threats. The slightest hint of danger is enough to cause panic. That moment had arrived and the children attacked. Several hurled spears. Others ran after their quarry, hoping for a chance to strike.

Unseen, Morgana had taken an unusual route to her destination. From the stack, she set out past the lake and then headed north over the forest. When she reached the river, she followed it upstream towards Carw. Just before the settlement, Morgana banked to the right when she reached the edge of the woodland. She saw three startled deer, heading for open ground. They were closely pursued by two children.

In their excitement, all caution was abandoned. Both saw the dragon too late. A boy was snatched up. The girl alongside him had the good sense to throw herself to the ground. She heard the dragon's tail as it lashed out just above her. Clinging on to the boy, Morgana turned sharply in an attempt to kill the girl. She had leapt to her feet as soon as Morgana had swept over her and just made it to the safety of the trees. She felt the rush of heat as foliage was set alight behind her. Screaming, she continued to run deep into the woods.

The few people outside at Carw were alerted to the danger. The dragon's roar caused chaos. Everyone rushed to seek safety. One woman held her hands over her ears, seeking to block out the fiendish sound. Terrified and in agony, the boy was helpless. He watched as the meeting house swung into view. Suddenly, he felt the claws of the dragon open. He tumbled about thirty paces and struck the roof. He crashed through the turf, the animal skins and the rafters of pine. Still alive, he then fell the short distance to the meeting house floor.

He landed on the earth with a thump, narrowly missing two old women gutting some fish. To the amazement of all inside, the boy then stood up and promptly fainted with shock. Blood oozed out of the wounds around the tops of his shoulders.

Morgana continued to roar as she swept over the settlement, seeking anyone still outside. She attempted to set fire to the roofs of several roundhouses, with little success. She was not satisfied with her day's work and decided to play a waiting game. She came in to land midway between the settlement and the woods. She kept the river directly behind her. From her safe vantage point, she commanded an excellent view of the enemy on both flanks.

In the woods, panic reigned. Several of the smaller

children had to be held back from running home. Some were crying. Others had run deep into the woods, where new dangers lay in wait. Olin decided to take control. He shouted at the top of his voice. "Stand still and listen to me."

He grabbed one young boy running past him and told him to settle down. "Listen to me. If we stay in the woods, we are safe. We need to keep together and hold our nerve." Olin signalled to two of the older girls and a boy. "A few of us have run into the woods. You three, follow them and try to bring them back. Take spears and stay together. Eoin and Anwar, I have a job for you two."

Anwar grinned. "I know. You want us to climb a tree and tell you what the dragon is doing."

"That's right. Can you do that for me?"

"All right. We will let you know what is going on shortly."

They glanced around for a suitable tree. It needed to have a wide crown to provide protection from above. It needed to be a high tree to keep the dragon at bay. Above all, it needed to be a tree they could flee from in a hurry. No discussion took place. Eoin pointed to a large tree about forty paces from the edge of the woods. Anwar nodded and they trotted to its base.

The two climbed up high enough to be able to see the dragon. Eoin shouted down to Olin. "We can see him now. He's on the ground by the river, about halfway between these woods and the settlement."

"What's the dragon doing?"

Neb would have been proud of Eoin's brief reply.

"He must be doing something."

"No. He is just sat there, doing nothing."

"Fine. Keep watching him. Let me know if anything happens."

Morgana could hear the shouting in the woods. She knew they were safe if they sheltered under the trees. She decided to wait a little while longer.

By now, the children who had run deep into the woods had all been rounded up. Olin decided to keep them busy. "I think the dragon will go home long before it gets dark. If we have to stay the night here, we need to build a fire and lay the ground."

The youngest children were asked to gather up any dry wood they could find. The rest were asked to drag back any branches of thorn or large logs that would help them to build a refuge. Apart from the activity in the woods, nothing happened for quite some time. Everyone at Carw stayed indoors. The dragon remained by the riverbank.

In the meeting house, Corsen was tending to the young boy's wounds. He had a clutch of injuries. First, she treated the wounds in his shoulders. She washed the claw marks and then smeared the gaping holes with honey. Next, she removed several large splinters from his legs. These too were coated in honey and then bandaged with skins. Finally, she examined his chest. She decided that only time could heal the heavy bruising and damage to his ribs.

The boy was also suffering from shock and severe concussion. He drifted in and out of consciousness, moaning about the pain and the dragon. Corsen spoke to the boy's mother. "I have done everything I can. Try to get him to drink a little water. If he is still alive tomorrow morning, he has a fighting chance."

Outside, the impasse continued. Finally, Morgana grew hungry and chose to head south for lunch. She stood up and stretched out her wings. When she was ready, she took flight towards the coast. From their eyrie, Eoin and Anwar carefully watched her progress. When they were certain she had gone, Eoin shouted down to Olin.

"The dragon's left. He has flown south. Do you want to make a run for it?"

"Yes, let me get everyone ready at the edge of the woods. I want to know that the dragon is still out of sight." Eoin nodded.

All the children were herded towards the edge of the woodland. Olin shouted once more to Eoin. "Is it still all clear?"

Eoin waved. "Yes, Anwar and I are going to stay here, climbing trees. Now, run like the wind."

The two watched as the line of children flowed down the slope towards safety.

CHAPTER 52
Storm Clouds

Although winter was not far away, southerly warm air continued to stream towards the coast. The benign weather was about to end. Beyond the river, cold winds were pushing down from the north. Teilo was the first to forecast the coming of the storm. He delighted in seeking out Menw. He pointed to the dark clouds building to the north-west. "Menw, there's a storm on the way and I think we are going to be hit by it."

Menw confessed that he had not yet spotted the threat. Teilo slapped him on the back. "Don't worry. When I have some time, I will teach you the signs." The boy was quick enough to evade the old man's playful blow.

That night, a lone gannet swept in towards land on the temperate, southerly breeze. Under a full moon, the large seabird could now make out his destination. The old gannet had survived over thirty winters, on sea and cliffs. Weary from the long flight, he was looking forward to resting a while. When the sun was up, he would feed on the abundant shoals of fish near to the coast.

The gannet secured landfall at the earliest opportunity. He landed on a large stack of limestone, near to the cliffs. As was his wont, he signalled his arrival with a harsh, grating call. He was not aware that a dragon was asleep, less than three paces behind him. The bird's screech woke Morgana with a start. Fearing she was under attack, she obliterated the imaginary threat before her. The unfortunate gannet plummeted to the sea below in a ball of flame.

Morgana was now fully awake. She looked towards the east. The first signs of dawn glowed on the horizon. Today was an opportunity to pay an early visit to Carw. She headed due north over the forest. When she saw the silvery stretch of water, she dropped down low and followed the river. For the people of Carw, her timing was catastrophic.

Nearby, three groups were out in the open. On the river, Eyslk and two other women were checking the traps. Mabon was leading a hunting party of seven men. Fifteen children were following about fifty paces behind.

The first people Morgana saw were the women on the river. She was about to begin her attack when she caught sight of the two larger groups to the right. She turned towards Mabon's hunting party. They immediately knew they were too far from safety. Wisely, they scattered in several directions. Mabon and two others tried to run to the woods. Three men ran back towards Carw, shouting at the children to seek safety. Strangely, one man sprinted straight towards Morgana's line of attack.

The hunter who headed to the river was in luck. By running so quickly, he managed to pass underneath Morgana before she could lose enough height to bring him in range. She tried to swat him with her tail, but narrowly missed. Mightily relieved, the man reached the safety of a building near to the riverbank.

Morgana turned her attention to the three men heading for the woods. Mabon had shouted at the other two to spread out. Mabon was nearest to the tree line. As the other two manoeuvred to the right and left, they lost a little ground. The three were now about twenty paces apart. Morgana had nimbly turned back towards the river. She lined up Mabon and the hunter to his left. Both were struck by the whip-like action of her tail. Mabon died instantly of a broken neck. His companion died later that day. The third man managed to reach the safety of the trees.

Morgana turned right towards the settlement. She closed in on her victims with remarkable speed. There was still a handful of people who had not reached the edge of Carw when Morgana struck. The first to die was one of Mabon's hunters. He had badly twisted his ankle as he tried to flee. His injury sealed his fate. Morgana crashed him with her tail as she swept overhead. He was knocked off his feet and died when he struck the wall of a roundhouse.

Two children were enveloped in flame moments before reaching the nearest building. A young woman was killed by the dragon's vicious tail. Morgana swept past the settlement and turned again. Nobody remained outside. Most shuddered with fear as she roared her defiance.

About thirty people had sought refuge in the meeting house. There was blind panic when they heard the dragon on the ridge of the roof. Morgana had deliberately landed with a thump to test its strength. Luckily, Alawn had insisted on a very thick ridge beam when the meeting house was built. The timber creaked but held her weight. She bounced up and down, seeking to bring down the roof. The beam groaned again but held firm.

Next, she tried to burn out her prey. Using her claws, she tore away a large patch of turf from the roof and dragged out the animal skins below. Now, only the pine rafters running from the ridge beam to the long walls of the building offered any protection. She could hear the screaming below. With one foot on the ridge beam, she smashed several of the rafters by stamping on them.

Taking great care not to overbalance, she poked her head through the hole. Nobody was directly below her. She could see the terror on the faces of the occupants, pressed up against both gable walls. She flooded fire through the hole, trying to burn down the building from within. All felt the surges of heat as fireballs were blasted in from above.

From a roundhouse nearby, two hunters had seen Morgana's antics on the roof. They decided that they had to do something. Their plan was simple. They would carry a spear in their throwing hand and two spares in the other. They would run at full tilt towards the meeting house and each hurl a spear at the dragon. If they survived, they would seek shelter inside. If they got the chance, they would throw their two spares from within the building. It was foolhardy, yet no other option presented itself.

The two wished each other luck and broke cover. Busy on the roof, Morgana did not see their approach. She looked down just in time to see them launch their spears. She had no time to evade the attack. Both spears found their mark. One weapon bounced off her. The other inflicted some damage, ploughing through a narrow gap in her scales. She roared in shock and pain.

Moments later, another spear shot upwards through the hole in the roof. This struck her knee, causing further agony.

Fearing for her own safety, Morgana decided it was time to leave. When she was recovered, she would return to Carw once more and kill again. In much discomfort, she set off for home.

Beyond Freshwater Beach, thick clouds were building at a rapid rate. The wind had shifted and a cold front was clashing with the warmer southerly air. The swirling air masses meant that a violent thunderstorm was inevitable. Out to sea, lightning was already pulsing through the heavy, black clouds.

Morgana had not seen the coming of the storm. Her first warning was the rumble of thunder in the distance. It was only on her flight home that she realised the full extent of the threat. She decided to take the shortest route. With luck, she could take shelter before the worst of the storm swept over the cliffs.

CHAPTER 53

An Act of Faith

On the cliffs, Teilo was anxious to witness the ferocity of the storm. Menw warned him about the power of nature. Teilo was insistent. "If we shelter in the work shed, we will be able to see over the earthworks. If you are too scared, I will go alone."

Ysperin was also keen to see the storm. Together, they persuaded the old man to join them. When they started to put on weather skins, Mair wanted to know why they were venturing outside in such awful weather. Reluctantly, Ysperin explained their plan.

"Can I come? I love thunder and lightning." She waved her arms about and made strange, crashing noises.

Behind her, Vala was laughing. "Watch out, Mair. I reckon you have already been struck by lightning. Next time, you may not be so lucky."

Mair was confused. "I do not remember being hit by lightning. Are you sure? I think I would have remembered." As if to prove Vala's point, she played with her wild hair.

Ysperin threw a weather skin towards the old woman. "If you are coming, hurry up. The storm is almost overhead."

The work shed was an ideal place to observe the passing

of the storm. In the eastern wall, there was an open window just below the eaves of the roof. This gap in the wall allowed light and air into the store. Standing on a bench, the four had an excellent view over the earthworks.

The storm was moving in at great speed. The thunder and lightning grew ever nearer. Teilo was surprised by how cold he felt as heavy rain drenched the coastal plain. Morgana flew as quickly as she could muster. Her plan was to sweep over the cliffs and land on her stack as soon as possible.

When she reached home, she felt she would be safe. Her lair was below the nearby cliffs. If she lay low in the hollow at the top of the stack, she would be protected by the shield of stone around her. She was now less than two thousand paces from home. Teilo spotted her first as she battled her way through the high winds and driving rain.

The storm was at its height. Morgana was just about to turn for home when she was struck by an explosion of sound. The thunder burst perforated both her eardrums. The shockwaves from the lightning flash temporarily blinded her. Disorientated and in great pain, she landed heavily in the heather.

Ysperin sensed she was now in great danger. Before Menw could stop him, he ran out of the work shed, grabbing a spear by the entrance. He scrambled up the slippery earthworks and thrust his spear towards the heavens. "Look out!"

The three stood behind him barely heard his cry, as it was almost lost in the wind and rain. At the moment he yelled out, a bolt of lightning struck Morgana a mortal blow. Her heart could not bear the huge surge of energy that flowed through her body. The four watched as her legs buckled and she rolled onto her side.

Mair was convinced that it was Ysperin who had killed the

dragon. His cry on the earthworks was a threat, not a warning. He had summoned the lightning with his spear. For the few winters left to her, Mair did nothing to upset the boy. When Ysperin asked her to do something for him, she promptly did so without complaint. When her visits to Flat Rock resumed, she confided in Nesta. She, too, believed the boy held sway over the elements. "Thank Ysperin he was there to save us from the dragon."

Early next day, Gleis led out the entire settlement to inspect the fallen dragon. Overnight, wolves had tried to gnaw at the carcass, with limited success. Few spoke as they stood and stared. Ysperin fought back the tears as he briefly placed his hand on Morgana's head. Finally, Gleis, Adain and several others headed straight for Carw. When they arrived, the settlement was deserted. In time, the people were coaxed outside and the celebrations to mark their deliverance began in earnest.

Gleis always remembered Addolgar's expression when he delivered the good news. Before winter set in, the roof of the meeting house was repaired and life's struggles continued in a quieter vein. With the death of Morgana, the extraordinary suddenly became commonplace. No more is known of the souls at Carw or on the cliffs, as the end of their stories has long been lost in the mists of time.

Several millennia ago, the daily battle between man and auroch finally ended on Gleis's old hunting grounds. Their distant cousins now roam on open pastureland where the forest once stood. Beef cattle and milking cows continue to feed us. To this day, we still make use of their hides for clothing.

All living things have their day and only the landscape remains to be shaped by time. Since those early days, so much has changed. A few signposts from the distant past, however, are still with us. On the coast, Pebble Bay and Dead Man's Leap are still there, albeit with different names. At Pebble Bay, children now gambol in the surf where Morgana once relieved the pain in her claws.

Cadwr's sinkhole is still there, if you care to seek it out among the heather and gorse. If you walk west to where wild horses used to steer clear of all living things, you will reach Freshwater Beach, now known as Freshwater West.

Morgana's lair is now little more than a stump of rock. New stacks nearby have formed. They too are constantly being shaped by the timeless forces of nature. The finger of land on which Gleis's settlement was sited is still there. To the trained eye, the earthworks can just be made out. They, too, have been worn down by the elements.

Inland, the river still meanders past where Carw once stood. An abandoned castle sits by the water. Trees still grow in woodland where Eoin and Anwar plied their trade. Today, at the village of Carew, an old Cross stands by the roadside. It was only hauled into place about a thousand years ago. The carved stone is a recent pointer in time. The rear of the Cross looks back to where the ancient settlement once stood.

As we reach the end of this tale, the question you ask me is this. Did Morgana and her kind really exist? In reply, I ask the same question of you. Without proof, belief is simply an act of faith. I know what I believe but like Eus and Sel long before me, I am just a messenger. This is the story that was handed down to me. I now entrust it to you. Make of it what you will.

THE END

ABOUT THE AUTHOR

John Roberts grew up on a farm with his two brothers in Pembrokeshire. He graduated from Leeds Polytechnic with an honours degree in business studies. Thereafter, he worked throughout his career in various marketing posts for British Gas.

Now retired, he is a keen golfer. His main pastimes are sport, travel and reading. He lives in Leeds with his wife, Mary. This is his first novel.

Printed in Great Britain
by Amazon